<u>*Dedication*</u>

This book is dedicated to <u>Volunteers</u>. Our country has thousands of communities; some are small towns and some are large cities. Every thriving community has a myriad of volunteer organizations.

Volunteer organizations strive to: '<u>enrich & improve</u>' the lives of those that they serve. Volunteer organizations only succeed, if they have an abundance of 'dedicated volunteers.'

Some Volunteer organizations are well known & International organizations - such as, The Red Cross and Habitat for Humanity. It would be impossible for me to list every Volunteer Organization that exists, but I will list some ways that people volunteer. This list includes: the 'Blood Bank donors' & blood drive volunteers, the Volunteer Firefighters and their auxiliary groups, The Boy Scout & Girl Scout leaders, The Youth Sports Coaches, The Boys & Girls Club Mentors & Volunteers, The PTA members (including the cake sale bakers, room mothers and fundraising volunteers), The Humane Society volunteers, The Environmental Cleanup groups, The Church volunteers (including the Choir singers, ushers, Bible school teachers, and cookie & cake sale bakers), The Animal Rescue volunteers (including those who transport animals and those who foster animals - until they are adopted), The Food Pantry Volunteers, The Student Youth Organizations - like The Key Club, etc.

The list of Volunteer Organizations and Civic Organizations is endless. My personal passions are the Environmental Organizations and the Organizations that aid the 'Poor & Needy' - especially those who are in need of food.

Volunteers enable our communities to thrive - they make our towns more 'vibrant.' Volunteer Organizations bring diverse groups of people (people from a variety of ethnicities) together --- working for a common purpose.

There aren't any age restrictions to volunteering - the 'very young' and the 'very old' can and do --- volunteer. I've seen young children selling lemonade (along the bike path, that is near where I live); these youngsters raise money for the Humane Society, Cancer needs and other charitable needs. I also know people who are in their 90's that volunteer in their communities.

Volunteering makes our world Better --- little by little!

Every 'Little bit' - of volunteering --- Helps!

Please, Volunteer?! When you do, you will feel - 'more beautiful inside!'

"Simply Good Readings for All" --- is available for purchase on Amazon.com

<u>Foreword</u>

The writings in this volume are designed to brighten your day and warm your heart. The stories (in Volume 6), will illustrate the '<u>beautiful side</u>' of Nature and Human Nature.

These stories involve the 'Childhood Experiences' of two little brothers. The older brother was frequently doing things that were - not too smart; he was often in trouble. The younger brother had a 'unique connection' - to Nature. You will 'Smile' as you read about the little brother; you will shake your head - (in wonderment), as you read about the actions of the older brother.

These stories were experienced long ago - in a small town. Some of the activities that these little boys engaged in - are still enjoyed today --- by 'Children' & the 'Young - at - Heart.'

It is the writer's hope that these stories will encourage the readers to: <u>explore</u> Nature. It is also the writer's hope that the readers of these stories will learn to: '<u>see the many good & beautiful things</u>' - that are all around us. Our daily life is 'filled with beauty.' Let these writings enable you to '<u>see</u>' - <u>how beautiful & exciting life is</u>. Yes, life is 'exciting' - to all 'Explorers.' It doesn't matter if you are 8 years old or 80 years old - all explorers - 'see with joy-filled eyes.' All explorers let Nature teach them how: '<u>to live</u>.' Nature has all of the answers - explorers & the 'Young - at - Heart' --- know this.

Let these stories enable you to 'see & experience' the 'Joys of Life.' Make time and take time to EXPLORE --- '<u>LOOK & SEE</u>' and '<u>be in AWE</u>' of <u>Nature</u>. Explore with your loved ones; learn to 'see' - 'Natural Beauty' --- in tiny little places & things. Let Nature improve your Nature.

Create 'loving memories' with your loved ones, as you explore the 'Natural Beauty' - that is all around you. And as you create loving memories, remember the Indian proverb: "We do NOT inherit the land from our ancestors, we borrow it from our children." As you journey through life, teach your family & all - 'How to care for Planet Earth.' Let these writings make you feel --- 'more beautiful inside!'

"Hometown Treasures"

Table of Contents

1. Introduction

This book is a continuation of the exploits and adventures of two brothers. In the previous book (Volume 5), the two brothers spent many days on the beach of a barrier island. While enjoying the beach and their time swimming in the ocean, the younger brother discovered several treasures. The younger brother also learned that he had a 'unique connection,' to nature. In addition, the younger brother learned that he 'possessed,' unique gifts or traits.

These two brothers were only one year apart in age; but they were very different. The older brother (named Zack) was an 'Alpha;' he was a 'rough & tough' boy. He often was in trouble and doing things that got him into trouble. The younger brother (named Zeke) was an 'Omegan;' he was quiet, shy and obedient.   Adults, who knew these brothers, would often say: --- that they were 'totally opposite.'

As stated above, Zeke discovered several treasures while he was at the beach. Zeke also encountered many unique people, while he was exploring on this barrier island. These 'unique individuals' could see - that Little Zeke was 'special.' One of these 'unique individuals,' told Zeke what his gifts were and that the island would give its many treasures to Zeke; because he was 'special' and had a 'special connection' to nature. Little Zeke learned that Nature was counting on him to aid it and help it survive.

Some of the treasures that Zeke discovered, he gave away. Some treasures were given to his favorite aunt. Some treasures were given to a unique individual named Ben. Ben was called 'Benevolent Ben,' or the 'Pearl Man.' Ben was always helping and aiding those who needed help; especially children who were in the hospital - being treated for cancer.

There were two island treasures that Zeke always carried with him. Zeke always carried: 1) the skeleton key (that had an Omega symbol on it), and 2) the green sea glass (it magnified objects, whenever Zeke looked through it). Little Zeke also always wore his 'good luck' necklace that he found on the beach. Zeke learned that his necklace was made of 'special beads' and that the Indians (who visited the beach long ago) wanted him to have it.

When Zeke was little, he had to play outside with his bigger brother (Zack). Zeke would listen to his older brother, and do whatever he told him to do; but that often led to trouble. In this volume of stories, the readers will see some of the predicaments that Zack (Zeke's older brother) got into. This volume of stories will also continue the journey of a 'special' little boy - named Zeke.

In this volume, Zeke discovers more treasures and he encounters more 'unique individuals.' Zeke realizes that his hometown has many treasures. Zeke also uses his 'unique innate gifts' - to aid Nature and others. Zeke also meets - 'the thing' --- that lived under the jetty on the barrier island beach (where Zeke and Zack spent many summer days with their parents).

Enjoy these 'heart - warming' stories. You might want to reread Volume 5 (before reading Volume 6). If you reread volume 5, you will really see how beautiful Nature is and how connected we all are to Nature. HAPPY READING!

****

2.   The Woods Are on Fire

Long ago, parents would often send their children outside to play. Most children would play outside all day. Zack and Zeke were like all of the other children in their neighborhood. If it wasn't a school day, Zeke's mom would always say: "Zack and Zeke, go outside and play." Zack's mom wanted quiet time, so she would send Zack and Zeke outside. Remember, Zack was child #6, and Zeke was child #7. There NEVER was any 'quiet time' when Zack was inside with his brother --- these two brothers were always fighting (annoying each other).

Zeke was the youngest child in the family. Zeke's mom would tell Zack to watch Zeke and to take care of him (when they were outside - playing). Big brothers are supposed to 'protect' their little brothers. Zack didn't want to protect his little brother. Zack didn't even want to play with his little brother. Zack wanted to play with the older kids, who lived in the neighborhood. But Zeke was always told (by his mother), "to stay with his older brother, whenever they were outside playing."

Zeke's mom made Zeke stay with his older brother (when she sent them outside to play), because Zeke got lost on the beach when he was 4 years old. Zeke had a tendency to wander off and explore; or maybe he was just trying to get away from an older brother who was always punching him and annoying him.

One sunny day, Zack and Zeke were outside playing with several of the neighborhood children. One of these (older neighborhood) kids was like Zack; she was often in trouble. She was often doing something that she shouldn't be doing. This girl was a few years older than Zack and she was a 'trouble-maker.' The younger (neighborhood) kids would always listen to this girl. The little kids would always do whatever she asked them to do. All of the little kids were afraid of this 'bossy girl.'

One day this girl said to Zack, "Let's go play in the woods behind my house. I want to show you something." Zack couldn't resist. Zack did whatever this girl suggested; she was older than Zack and Zack was happy - just to be playing with an older kid. Zeke had to stay with his bigger brother, whenever he was outside playing; so Zeke followed Zack and this older girl into the woods (that were behind their houses).

The woods behind Zack and Zeke's house was an undeveloped block. There weren't any homes on that tract of land. The woods were fun to play in. All of the neighborhood kids would go into this tract of wooded land and look for snakes, turtles and frogs. In the Spring, tadpoles were often caught in the small ponds in these woods.

On this summer day (when Zeke was about 4 years old), Zeke followed his big brother Zack and the older 'bossy' girl into the woods. It hadn't rained in a long time, so the tall weeds and grasses in the woods were very dry. As soon as we got to the woods, the older 'bossy' girl said to Zack, "Look what I have." She reached into her pocket and took out a pack of matches. Then the older girl said to Zack, "Watch me light these matches."

My brother (Zack), knew that we weren't supposed to play with matches. All little children were told, "DON'T PLAY with Matches!" This older girl was often doing what she was told 'not to do'; she was a lot like Zack --- she often didn't behave and do what her parents told her - 'to do.'

On this day, this 'bossy' girl was having a lot of fun. She was lighting one match after another. She would toss the matches onto the ground (after she lit them); thinking that they were out. Unfortunately, one or some of those matches weren't out (they reignited). Within a few minutes, we saw the tall grass catching on fire.

All of us knew that this was bad. We knew that we shouldn't be playing with matches. We knew that we had to quickly 'put the fire out.' And we knew that we would be in: 'BIG TROUBLE;' if we didn't put the fire out.

Being the littlest one there, I quickly said to my bigger brother, "Zack! What should I do?" Zack said, "Throw the newspapers (that were lying nearby in the grass) on it." I listened to my older brother and threw newspapers onto the fire. It didn't put the fire out.

The woods quickly went up in flames. We quickly ran across the street and banged on the front door (of the nearest house). As we were banging on the door, we were yelling: "The Woods are on Fire! The Woods are on Fire! HELP! HELP!"

The neighbors called the Fire Company and the Firemen came and put the fire out. No houses were burned or damaged, but we knew that we were in: 'Trouble, if our parents found out that we were playing with matches.'

We played the rest of the day hoping that our Dad wouldn't find out. We knew that we would be in: 'Big Trouble' - if our dad found out. We would be 'Spanked!' We also knew that the older girl would be beaten with a 'horse strap' - if her dad found out that she was playing with matches and set the woods on fire.

Later (that day), while playing in front of my house, my next door neighbor came home. Mr. Henry is my favorite neighbor and the nicest man. Mr. Henry (my neighbor) got out of his car and yelled to me, "Zekie, I was listening to my Police Scanner radio and heard that some children were playing with matches and that they set the woods on fire. They mentioned two names that I know. One child was named Zack and one was named Zeke." Then Mr. Henry said, "Zeke, you're going to get a 'whoopin' (a spanking), when your dad gets home from work. You better go and hide in the attic - until he cools down (gets less angry)." Zeke responded, "Mr. Henry, I wasn't playing with matches. I was just there, with my brother. I have to stay with my brother when I'm outside playing. Veedie was playing with matches; she set the woods on fire. I just did what my big brother told me. Zack told me to throw newspapers on the fire. He said it would smother the fire and put it out. So I threw newspapers on it and the fire got bigger."

Mr. Henry was laughing (out loud), when he heard Zeke say: 'that he threw newspapers onto the burning grass.' Mr. Henry then said, "Zekie, I believe you but NEVER throw newspapers onto a fire - unless you want the fire to get bigger; newspaper is kindling - it is used to 'start a fire.' Again, Zekie - I know how mad your dad can get; you better hide in the attic until he calms down." Zeke responded, "OK Mr. Henry, I will hide in the attic. There's a tiny corner in the attic that my dad won't go into, because it's dark and covered with cobwebs and spiders. My dad doesn't like cobwebs or spiders and there aren't any lights in our attic, so he won't be able to see me (hiding in the attic). Thanks Mr. Henry - for telling me that newspapers are used for kindling (to start fires); I didn't know."

****

3.   The Hornets' Nest

The next day, Zeke's mom sent Zack and Zeke outside to play. But before she let them go outside, Zeke's mom said, "Zack, don't get into any trouble. Don't play with any matches and don't play with Veedie. Find something to do that won't get you into trouble. You are the bigger brother, so take care of Zeke." Zack responded, "Okay Mom!"

As soon as Zack and Zeke got outside, they saw a neighborhood boy named Ernie. Zeke said to Ernie, "Ernie, do you want to play with us?" Ernie said, "Sure! But first, I have to make sure my horses have food and water. You and Zack can help me feed my horses, if you want." Zack yelled, "Sure! I like horses!"

Zack and Zeke quickly ran across the street to Ernie's house. Ernie's family and Veedie's family had horses in their backyards. Ernie's horses were nice but Veedie's one horse was wild; it was mean. All of the neighborhood children were afraid of it. One time, it kicked Mr. Henry's youngest daughter (Joyce) in the head.

While Ernie was feeding his horses, Zeke was talking 'softly & petting' one of Ernie's horses. Ernie's horse (named Betty), was very friendly. Betty came out of her stall and let Zeke pet her and rub her cheeks. Sometimes, Zeke would give Betty sugar cubes. Betty would eat 'sugar cubes' - right out of Zeke's hand.

Zeke didn't have a chance to feed Betty sugar cubes today, because Zack got himself --- into 'BIG TROUBLE!' While Zeke was petting Betty (Ernie's horse), Zack saw a large Hornets' Nest. The Hornets' nest was attached to and hanging from the barn rafters. Zack couldn't leave it alone. Zack is ALWAYS --- getting into trouble!

Zack yelled to Ernie, "Ernie I need a pole or long stick. I want to knock down the bees nest that's hanging in your barn." Ernie said, "I'm almost done feeding my horses; I'll get two poles to knock it down." Zeke said, "Zack, I don't think you should mess around with that Hornets' nest. Hornets, Wasps and Bees sting; you know that!" Zack responded, "I can run faster than the Hornets. As soon as I knock it down, I'll run out of the barn and the Hornets won't know where I'm at."

Ernie found two poles and gave one to Zack. Zack and Ernie started to 'poke' - at the Hornets' nest. Zeke saw lots of hornets coming out of the nest, when Zack 'poked' the nest. Zeke then said, "Zack, you better stop. The Hornets are getting mad; they're going to sting you!" Then Zack decided to show how 'strong' he was; he took the pole and swung really hard and knocked the Hornets' nest down.

As soon as the Hornets' nest was knocked down, dozens of Hornets went after Zack and Ernie. It seemed as if the Hornets knew who to attack - for destroying their nest. We all ran from the barn. Zack ran 'Super' fast, but he couldn't outrun the Hornets. Ernie only had to run 30 feet to his house. Ernie got stung three (3) times and he was crying like a baby; he was screaming! Zack and Zeke had to run 50 yards to their house. Zack was 'way-ahead' of Zeke and running fast to his house (when they exited the barn). Zeke was 'way-behind' his older brother, but the Hornets didn't sting Zeke. Amazingly, all of the Hornets flew past Zeke and decided to go after Zack and Ernie. Zeke didn't get stung; not even once.

Zack was screaming as he ran towards his house. He was yelling, "MOM! MOM! Help! Help!" When Zeke got to his house, Zack was being stung, repeatedly. Zeke's mom was on the porch; she was 'swatting' the Hornets with a broom. Zeke's mom kept swatting the Hornets off of Zack until she could get him inside and tend to his wounds.

Zack got stung by dozens of Hornets. Zeke's mom was stung a few times as she attempted to get the Hornets away from Zack. Once inside, Zeke's mom took care of Zack's wounds. Zack's mom covered each sting with 'Baking soda' paste. Zack looked weird, he was covered with 'white patches.' He had 'Baking Soda' paste - all over his body; his face, arms and legs were covered with 'Baking Soda' paste.

Zeke waited a few minutes for the Hornets to fly away (from his house), then Zeke walked in and said: "Mom! Is Zack OK? He and Ernie were 'swatting' at a Hornets' nest in Ernie's barn. Zack knocked it down and the Hornets went after him and Ernie." Zeke's mom responded, "I think Zack will be OK, but I'm going to keep him inside for the rest of today. If I keep him inside and watch him, I know that he won't get into any more trouble. Zekie, why don't you go outside and play, that way Zack can rest." Zeke responded, "OK mom." Then Zeke said, "Mom, I didn't get stung by any Hornets. The Hornets flew by me and went after Ernie and Zack. The Hornets must have known who destroyed their nest." Zeke's mom responded, "I'm sure you're right. Nature knows how to protect itself and who its enemies are. Zekie, you have a unique connection to Nature. Your brother is 'wearing me out;' go outside and play. Zeke responded to his mother by saying, "Mom, I'll be out front. I'll be tossing my ball against the steps."

While Zeke was outside (tossing his pink rubber ball against the steps), he kept thinking about what his mom had said. Zeke's mom said, "Zekie, you have a 'unique connection' to Nature." This made Zeke think about Mr. Hill, Mr. Ben, Nurse Coral and the fisherman on the jetty (who had a sick parakeet). Those people also told Zeke that he was 'special' and that Nature would lead him to its many treasures. Now, Zeke was thinking about exploring and finding new treasures.

Zeke knew that he couldn't do any exploring today. He had to stay in front of his house and play by himself. Tossing a ball against the front steps was always fun. Zeke spent many hours - just tossing a ball against the steps of his house and catching the ball --- as it bounced off of the steps. While tossing the ball (against the steps), Mr. Henry (Zeke's next door neighbor) pulled up and got out of his car.

Zeke yelled, "Hi Mr. Henry! You won't believe what Zack did today. Zack knocked down a Hornets' nest in Ernie's barn. Zack got stung. The Hornets chased Zack and stung him; he has: 'red welts,' all over his body. The Hornets didn't sting me at all - not even once." Mr. Henry responded, "Your brother Zack is ALWAYS into some kind of trouble. I don't know how your mom can put up with him everyday. I don't know how she does it. Your mom has the patience of Job." Zeke responded, "Mr. Henry, I don't know Job; does he live nearby?" Mr. Henry laughed then said, "Zekie, you are a blessing to your mom! Keep being the 'nice little boy' that you are." Zeke responded, "Mr. Henry, you're my favorite neighbor; thanks for calling me 'nice;' I try to be nice to everybody."

****

*Fortunately, Zack wasn't allergic to insect stings (Bees, Wasps or Hornets). He did recover from the dozens of Hornet stings that day. True story; the Hornets really didn't sting Zeke. Nature does seem to know --- who its friends & aiders are. Read on and see what Zeke discovers, and learns - about Nature & people.

4.   The Candy Man

While Zack was inside (resting & recovering from the dozens of Hornet stings), Zeke was outside. Zeke was throwing a rubber ball against the steps of his house; he loved to 'throw & catch' balls. While Zeke was throwing & catching his ball, a neighborhood boy yelled to him, "Zeke, do you want to play catch with me?" Zeke instantly responded, "Sure, Billy!" Then Zeke yelled to his mom, "Mom! I'm going across the street to play with Billy; is that OK?" Zeke's mom responded, "Sure! Billy is a nice boy; you can play with him anytime you want."

Billy lived a few houses away from Zeke. He was a year older than Zeke but he and Zeke got along very well. Unlike Zeke, Billy didn't have any brothers or sisters; he was the 'only child' - in his family. Billy's mom was 'very protective' - she worried about him. Billy lived with his mother, father and grandmother. Zeke's mom didn't worry about Zeke; she had seven (7) children. Zeke was the youngest of seven kids; Zeke's mom didn't have time to worry about Zeke - she had to 'survive' each day. Every day 'mothering' Zack - was an adventure.

Little Zeke ran across the street to Billy's house. Zeke said to Billy, "Get your baseball glove; then we can play 'pitch & catch." Billy said "OK!" Billy got his glove and said to Zeke, "I have a piece of chalk; let me draw a 'home plate' on the sidewalk. Zeke, you can be the 'Pitcher' and I'll be the 'Catcher.' Zeke responded, "OK Billy!"

Zeke loved to 'pitch' (throw baseballs). Zeke and Billy were having lots of fun, just 'throwing and catching' the rubber ball. Zeke would 'wind up' (like a major league pitcher) then throw the ball to Billy. Billy would catch each 'pitch' then respond - 'Strike or Ball.' Zeke and Billy pretended that they were (Battery mates - pitcher & catcher). They pretended that Zeke was 'striking out' imaginary batters.

While they were playing 'catch,' Billy's neighbor yelled, "You two are really good! Billy, you're a good 'Catcher' and Zeke is a good 'Pitcher;' Zeke's a 'South-Paw,' too." Billy responded, "Thanks, Uncle Eddie! Uncle Eddie do you have any extra candy - for us?" Eddie (Billy's neighbor) responded, "I do have some candy, you and Zeke can have some; stop over - when you're ready." Billy looked at Zeke, then said, "Let's go get some candy from Uncle Eddie."

Uncle Eddie brought out a bag of candy then said, "Billy, you and Zeke can help yourself to a few pieces of candy; don't take too much or it might ruin your appetite. I know that your parents don't want you to eat a lot of candy before dinner." While Zeke and Billy were selecting candy to eat, Eddie said: "Zeke, you're a 'South-paw;' you're a 'Lefty.' There aren't many good 'Left - handed' pitchers. You have really good 'mechanics' and 'good control' of your pitches; you could become a good pitcher when you get bigger. I was a 'Lefty' when I was little - like you --- long ago; but the teachers and adults didn't like 'Lefties.' Long ago, people made all little kids write with their 'right' hands. People used to think that 'Left - handedness' was evil. Teachers forced all students to write - using their 'right hand.'

There were lots of 'myths' long ago. Adults and parents would scare children with myths; one myth (told to kids long ago, was that 'left-handedness' was evil or from the devil). Today, we know that being 'left-handed' is fine. Science has shown and taught us that we get 'traits' or qualities from our parents. Being 'Left-handed' is a trait; having curly hair is also a trait." Zeke responded, "Uncle Eddie, you are bald; is being bald a trait that your parents gave you?" Eddie responded, "Yes, it is. When you and Billy get bigger, you can study 'Genetics' and learn all about 'traits' - qualities that are given to us from our parents."

Before leaving Eddie's house, Zeke asked Eddie: "Uncle Eddie, is being 'nice' a trait that you get from your parents? You are really Nice! And you have the 'Greenest lawn' - in the whole town! How do you make your grass so green and thick? Thanks for the Candy!" Eddie responded, "You and Billy are nice little boys and good friends. Being 'nice' is not a 'trait' that you get from your parents. All people can be - <u>NICE</u>! <u>Kindness</u> is a 'learned trait;' children are taught how to be 'kind.' My parents taught me to treat everyone with: 'Respect,' - even if they are mean to me. Your parents are teaching the two of you how to treat others. Keep being the 'Nice' little boys that you are and keep having fun - playing baseball. I loved playing Baseball, when I was little -

like you. One day, I will tell you how I make my lawn so green; I will also tell you about Mr. Henry. Zeke, you are very lucky: to have Mr. Henry as your neighbor; he is the perfect neighbor!"

When Zeke and Billy finished eating their candy, they walked across the street to Billy's house - to continue playing 'catch.' Before they resumed playing catch again, Zeke said to Billy: "Uncle Eddie is really nice! Why do all of the kids call him Uncle Eddie?" Billy responded, "Uncle Eddie is like an Uncle to all children. He doesn't have any children; he treats all of the neighborhood children like they are his own." Little Zeke responded, "OH. He is really nice and he always has candy. And he always shares his candy; he's very kind!"

****

*Long ago, being 'left-handed' was considered a 'curse' or the work of the devil. Fortunately, Science has proven that 'lefties' are equal to 'righties.' The writer writes with his right hand, but is a natural 'lefty'- a 'South-paw.' Teachers made the writer (of this book) learn how to write with his 'right' hand. The writer does some activities with his 'right' hand and some with his 'left;' maybe he's ambidextrous.
**Kindness is truly a learned trait --- everyone can be & should be: "<u>KIND</u>."
*** "Kindness is the language that the deaf can hear and the blind can see." - M. Twain

5.   The Screams in the Woods

The next morning, Zack had to stay inside and rest. Zack was still covered in 'red blotches' (from the dozens: of Hornet stings - on his body). Zeke's mom said to Zeke, "Zekie, go outside and play; you and Zack are always annoying each other - he needs to rest and I need 'peace and quiet.' It's never quiet or peaceful when you two are together." Zeke responded, "Ok mom, I'll go outside. Can I play with Billy, if he's allowed to come outside?" Zeke's mom replied, "Zeke, you can play with Billy anytime you want; he's such a nice boy and you two are becoming very good friends. I like Billy and I like you playing with him."

As soon as Zeke got outside of his house, he saw Billy across the street. Zeke yelled to Billy, "Billy, do you want to play with me today?" Billy responded, "Sure! Let's go exploring. Let's see if we can catch some turtles down by the creek. I'll bring my fishing net and a bucket. If we catch any turtles we can put them in my bucket."

While Billy was getting his net and bucket, Zeke went and asked his mom if he could go down to the creek with Billy. Zeke's mom said, "Zekie, you can go to the creek with Billy. Just be home at lunch time." Zeke responded, "OK. Thanks Mom!"

Zeke loved to explore and play in the nearby woods and in the creeks that were near his house. Catching turtles was always fun! Having a friend to 'play & explore' with was even - more fun!

As Zeke and Billy were walking to the creek, they talked about all of the animals that they thought they would see. Zeke said to Billy, "I bet we see lots of turtles sitting on logs today. It's really sunny today, so there should be lots of turtles out - sunning themselves." Billy responded, "I know we'll see lots of Turtles today, but we aren't going to catch any 'Stink-pots,' we're only going to catch: 'Spotted,' 'Painted' or Box Turtles."

As they walked to the nearby creek, Zeke's mind was 'racing & thinking' of finding some 'unique treasure.' Zeke had his two 'special treasures,' in his pocket. Whenever Zeke went exploring, he always had his: 'Green sea glass and his Skeleton key' in his pocket.

As soon as Billy and Zeke got to the creek, they saw several turtles. There were several turtles sitting on logs. Turtles often sit motionless on logs - on sunny days. Zeke learned that turtles sit on logs - to get the Algae off of their shells. The logs that turtles sit on are always floating in the water; the turtles want to be able to quickly get back into the water - if they are threatened.

As Zeke and Billy watched & counted the turtles that were sitting on the logs, the turtles were also watching Zeke and Billy. Billy knew that the turtles would dive back into the creek, if Zeke or Billy moved towards them.

As the turtles looked at Zeke, Billy said, "Zeke, I have a plan. Zeke, stay here. Let the turtles see you watching them; don't move - just keep staring at them. While the turtles are watching you, I'm going to sneak behind them. I'm going to 'sneak up' behind them and try to catch one in my net." Zeke responded, "That's a good plan. I'll keep staring at them and I won't move."

As soon as Billy started to walk away, (carrying his net), they heard screams! Zeke and Billy heard someone screaming! Someone was screaming, "HELP! HELP! Someone, PLEASE - HELP ME!"

Zeke and Billy instantly decided to go into the woods; catching turtles would have to wait. They quickly walked into the woods; they walked towards the 'loud screaming.' Within two minutes of walking (in the woods), they arrived at a tree. The tree had a 'deer stand' in it. The deer stand was like a partial 'tree house.' The 'deer stand' was twenty feet above the ground.   Hunters would often sit motionless in their deer stands - hoping that deer would walk underneath their stand. Deer didn't look up, so hunters could shoot deer - while sitting in their 'deer stands.'

When Zeke and Billy looked up into the 'deer stand,' they saw a boy. The boy was crying and yelling. He was yelling, "Please! HELP ME! My friends told me to climb up the rope ladder and stand in the 'deer stand.' When I got up the ladder they took away the ladder. They said that I should be brave; they said that I should show how brave I was. They wanted me to jump from the deer stand, into the creek. I'm afraid of heights and I can't swim very well. PLEASE! HELP ME! Help me get down!"

Zeke looked up, and saw how 'scared & frightened' the boy was. The boy was older than Billy and Zeke. He was much older than Zeke and Billy. Zeke yelled to the boy, "Billy and I will get you down; stop crying." Billy looked at Zeke and said, "I have a rope ladder; it's in my garage." Zeke responded, "Billy, run home and get your 'rope ladder.' I'll stay here and talk to the frightened boy; I'll try to calm him down."

When Billy ran home (to get his ladder), Zeke looked up into the deer stand and talked to the boy. Zeke kept telling him to: 'stay calm' and 'to breathe slowly.' Zeke's dad always told him: "Zeke, whenever you are afraid - close your eyes and breathe slowly." The boy (up in the tree), kept saying, "I'm afraid of heights! The kids made me climb this tree; they wanted me to prove that I was brave. I thought that they would be friends with me, if I climbed up to the deer stand."

As Zeke looked at the boy (who was stuck up in the tree), he saw a 'red mark' on the boy's face. Zeke decided to take out his 'green sea glass,' and look through it. Zeke's 'green sea glass,' was like a 'magnifier;' it made things look bigger and closer. When Zeke looked through the green sea glass, he saw the 'red skin patch' that was on the boy's face. Zeke instantly knew who the boy was.

Zeke looked up into the tree and said, "I know who you are. You are one of the 'Bullies' who stole my Halloween candy last year. You were one of the teenagers who were stealing Halloween candy from little kids. I know you were one of those 'mean kids.' You have the same 'birthmark' as my brother. My brother has that 'birthmark' - on his leg. When you stole my candy, I saw your 'red birthmark;' that was very mean of you to take candy from little kids. Even though you were mean to me, I'm going to help you get down from this tree. Just close your eyes and breathe slowly; don't look down. Billy will be back in a few minutes."

The boy looked at Zeke and said, "I'm sorry for taking your Halloween candy. I didn't want to do it. I just wanted to have some friends. No one wants to be my friend or play with me. Kids look at the 'red birthmark' on my face and they make fun of it. They call me names and laugh at me; I hate having this 'red skin patch' on my face. I just want to have a friend. I don't like being mean. You are lucky, you have a friend to play with; I don't have any friends. 'Bruiser the Bully' is the only person who will even talk to me. He said he would be my friend, if I climbed up this tree. When I got up in the tree he took away the ladder. Then he and the other boys laughed at me and called me names; they told me to be brave and jump into the creek. I started to cry and they really laughed at me; then they ran away and left me crying.

I'm really sorry for stealing your Halloween candy. I felt bad when I took your candy. You started crying, as soon as I took your candy. I saw how scared you were when I took your candy. I felt bad for days, but I just wanted a friend; so I did what the 'bully-boys' asked me to do."

Zeke responded, "That really was mean; I was 'Super-scared!' I cried all the way home. I feel sorry that you have that 'red birthmark' on your face; but you don't have to be mean. There are a lot of people who have 'birthmarks' and other physical handicaps. <u>There isn't any reason to be mean</u>. Mr. Hill told me that 'bullies' are often 'fear-biters.' He said that my brother is an 'Alpha;' - he's a 'fear biter.' I don't think that you are an 'Alpha' or a 'fear-biter,' but you are too old to play with Billy and me. My mom said that I have: 'the <u>gift of forgiveness</u>.' I forgive people who are mean to me. I don't hold grudges. My brother wouldn't forgive you. My brother would be mean to you. My brother believes in the saying: 'An eye for an eye.' If someone is mean to him, he will get them back; he will be mean to them. My brother is often in fights. My brother has a temper, he gets mad quickly. He will punch me whenever he gets mad, he punches me a lot.

I forgive you, for stealing my Halloween candy. But you don't have to be a 'bad boy' to get a friend. Billy and I will get you down from that tree; here comes Billy now."

When Billy walked up to Zeke, Zeke told Billy who the boy was. When Billy heard that he's the boy who stole Zeke's Halloween candy, Billy said: "We can't help him. He was mean to you; he made you cry. He's one of the Bully-boys." Zeke responded, "Billy, we have to help him; he's scared. It's the right thing to do. We should always help people who need help! I don't think that he is a bully. He has a 'red birthmark,' on his face and no one wants to play with him; kids make fun of him." Billy responded, "Ok, you're right; we should help anyone who needs help. I'll toss the rope ladder up to him."

The boy attached the rope ladder to the tree, then climbed down to the ground. As soon as he got on the ground he said, "THANKS, for getting me down. I'm sorry for being mean to you and taking your Halloween candy; I'll never do that again." Zeke responded, "I believe you, and I forgive you. I don't hold grudges like my brother, but you are too old to play with Billy and me. I think that I can find some 'nice' boys your age that you could become friends with." The boy responded, "Really? I would love to have a nice friend like yours."

Zeke looked at Billy and said, "This boy is old enough to be in the 'Boy Scouts.' Billy, your uncle is a 'Scout Leader.' You could ask your uncle to invite this boy to the next 'Scout' meeting." Billy responded, "That's a good idea. Everybody should have a friend to do things with. Zeke, you and I are best friends. I'll ask my uncle. I know that my uncle will help this boy." Billy looked at the boy and said, "The 'Boy Scouts' are nice boys, they will be nice to you. Would you like to join the Boy Scouts?" The boy responded, "I would, but I'm afraid. I won't know anyone. I'm shy!"

Billy said, "My uncle will take care of you and introduce you to a lot of nice boys. You'll meet a lot of nice boys, and surely will find friends to play with. Give me your phone number. I'll give my uncle your phone number and tell him to call your parents and tell them all about the Boy Scouts." The boy gave Billy his phone number and thanked Zeke and Billy again - for helping him.

As Zeke and Billy were walking home, Zeke said: "Billy, that was really nice of you to invite that boy to join the Scouts. I know that your uncle will help that boy find a friend. It is really sad that he has that 'birthmark,' on his face. It's also sad that some kids make fun of other kids; especially kids who 'look different' or are handicapped. Billy, you're really nice. I'm glad that you are my friend!"

****

*Mark Twain said, "Kindness is the language that the deaf can hear and the blind can see." He also said, "Forgiveness is the fragrance that the violet sheds on the heel that just crushed it." And Aesop said, "No act of kindness is ever wasted."

**<u>Kindness</u> & <u>Forgiveness</u> are: 'learned traits.' All people can learn to: 'be kind' and 'to forgive' - others.

***Unfortunately, there are 'bullies.' There are 'mean-spirited' people (i.e., bullies), who prey on people. Children who are different (e.g., one's with a handicap or birthmarks, and children who are timid), are often bullied. Some children, (like the boy who couldn't get down from the tree), will become bullies and do mean things. All children want to have a friend. It is the writer's belief that many bullies are: 'fear-biters;' they are afraid of not being liked --- so they bully others. As R. L. Stevenson said, "A friend is a gift that you give yourself." When people are 'kind' and learn to 'forgive,' they will gain friends; being a 'Bully,' will never get a person - 'friends.'

****Continue reading and see what happens to a 'Bully.'

6.   Bruiser the Bully

A Big Bruiser he be ---

and he left bruises, on all he did meet & see.

Read on and see - what Nature does --- to this bully!

After helping the 'boy who was bullied' down from the tree, Zeke and Billy walked back to Billy's house. It was near lunch-time, so they took the bucket and rope ladder back to Billy's house. Zeke asked Billy if he wanted to play after eating his lunch; Billy responded, "Sure! Come over to my house, after you eat your lunch; bring your glove --- we can play 'Pitch and Catch."

After lunch, Zeke and Billy played 'Pitch and Catch' and they played with Billy's dog. Billy has a 'Basset' hound dog; his dog's name is 'Tippy.' Tippy is a weird name, but Billy's dog is nice. Zeke would love to have a dog (for a pet), but Zeke's parents won't let him have a dog. Zeke's mom said, "Zekie, I have 7 kids to care for; I can't let you get a dog. It's exhausting, taking care of you and Zack; our parakeet (Smokey), is your pet. You can play with Billy's dog every day - if you want to."

Zeke and Billy decided that they would go back to the creek tomorrow. They both want to catch a turtle. The next day (after eating breakfast), Zeke asked his mom, "Mom, can I play with Billy today; and can we go down to the creek." Zeke's mom responded, "Zekie, you can play with Billy every day; and you can go down to the creek. You and Billy are becoming 'best friends;' he's such a nice boy. Make sure that you are home for dinner." Zeke responded, "Thanks Mom! We're going to try and catch some turtles." Zeke's mom responded, "Have fun, but don't bring home any snakes. I don't like snakes and your brother (Jeff) brought home a poisonous Copperhead snake once." Zeke responded, "Ok Mom; we'll only catch turtles."

When Zeke was crossing the street, he saw a shiny object lying in the road. Zeke bent down and saw that it was a 'quarter.' Zeke (instantly) felt like he had just discovered a 'treasure.' Remember, Zeke loved to explore; tiny little things were 'treasures' --- to Zeke.

As soon as Billy came out of his house (holding his net and bucket), Zeke said, "Billy, I just found a quarter in the street; let's stop at Breder's candy store. We can buy lots of penny candy. We can get a lot of candy with my quarter. The candy store is on the way to the creek." Billy responded, "Yeah! We can get a lot of penny candy with that quarter; thanks for sharing your quarter - with me."

Zeke and Billy each had a bag of 'penny candy.' They decided to sit and eat their candy by the creek. They planned on eating their candy as they watched the turtles; they knew that there would be lots of turtles. It was another sunny day, so the turtles would be sitting on logs.

Unfortunately, things changed. As soon as Zeke and Billy got to the creek, some teenagers approached them. The one 'Bully teenager' had his hat on 'back-wards;' this was his way of showing that he was 'cool.' His hat had letters on it. The letters: 'BtB' were stitched on it. Zeke tried to be nice and asked the big boy, "What does 'BtB' mean? I see those letters on your hat." The 'Bully teenager' said, "The letters stand for: 'Bruiser - the - Bully.' Everyone calls me that. I'm the toughest kid in town. Little boys, what do you have in those bags?" Zeke responded, "Billy and I have penny candy in our bags."

The 'Bully teenager,' then said to Zeke: "Give me your candy. I want all of your candy!" Zeke responded to the Bully-boy; Zeke said: "I'm not giving you all of my candy. If you had asked nicely, I would have shared my candy with you." The 'Bully' responded, "I'm not nice! I just take whatever I want; everyone is afraid of me!" Zeke

responded, "I'm not afraid of you. My brother (Zack), is a fighter; he will protect me."
The 'Bully' responded, "I know who Zack is; he's tough but he's a little kid. Zack is 7
years younger than me; he's a little kid - like you. Zack can't protect you from me."

Zeke responded to the 'Bully,' Zeke said: "My brother Jeff is in the Marines and
he is a great boxer. He will protect me from you. My other brother (Joe), is in the Navy,
he will protect me from you, too." The 'Bully' responded, "Your Marine brother and your
Navy brother aren't here now, to protect you --- so give me - all of your candy!" Zeke
responded, "No! Nature will take care of me. Nature will protect me from you. Nature
knows that Billy and I are nice; we always help Nature and people who need help."

The 'Bully' teen started to laugh at Zeke; he looked at his friends and they all
started to laugh at Zeke and Billy. Then, 'Bruiser the Bully' started to approach Zeke.
He reached out his hand and tried to take Zeke's bag of candy. Zeke quickly put his
candy bag into his pocket.

Then the 'Bully' said, "I'm going to rip it from your pocket. I'll rip your pants off, if
I need to. I always get what I want. Every kid in town is afraid of me." Zeke responded,
"I'm not afraid of you!"

As the 'Bully' reached for Zeke's pocket (in an attempt to take his bag of candy),
a hawk swooped down and took the 'Bully's hat.' Zeke couldn't believe it. A hawk
grabbed the 'Bully's hat;' then the hawk flew away (it flew up into a tree). The 'Bully's
hat was in the 'talons' (claws) of the hawk --- as it flew away.

The 'Bully' was really mad and upset; his face was 'beet red.' He clenched his
fist and started to scream at Zeke. He said, "That's my favorite hat; I never go
anywhere without that hat!" Then the 'bully' started to walk towards Zeke. Suddenly,
'little missiles' came flying out of the sky. The 'Bully' and his bully friends were being hit
in the head by 'little missiles.' Dozens of 'little missiles,' were being launched from the
trees. The 'bully-boys' were repeatedly hit with missiles. The 'bully-boys' ran away
from the creek; they instantly left Zeke and Billy.

Zeke looked up into the trees. He wanted to know who was launching 'missiles'
at the 'Bully-boys.' Zeke saw two squirrels; one squirrel was throwing acorns at the

'Bully-boys.' Another squirrel was dropping dozens of acorns on the 'Bully-boys.' The Flying squirrel had a dozen acorns (in its wings); it was dropping them on the 'bully-boys' - as it circled above them.

Billy looked at Zeke and said, "Zeke, I can't believe it; the hawk and those two squirrels just saved us from the Bully-boys." Zeke smiled and looked at Billy, then he said: "Nature will always aid and help those who help it survive. I am an 'Omegan;' I 'help & aid' Nature or anyone who needs help. Billy, you are an 'Omegan' too. Nature knows who its helpers are --- Nature will protect us, because we always try to protect it."

Zeke and Billy decided to walk home. Billy and Zeke had enough excitement for today. Catching turtles wouldn't happen today. Tonight, Zeke would be dreaming about Nature - being his protector!

****

*President Kennedy once said, "Children are our most valuable resource and our best hope for the future." Sadly, some children don't grow up and become 'assets' or 'valuable resources' - in their communities. Some children are bullied and become 'hopeless,' and some children become 'bullies.'

**All children should be treated as: 'valuable resources;' children deserve --- our best efforts. Someone once said: "You may only be one person in the world, but you might be 'the world' --- to one person." Therefore, try to make a positive difference - in someone's life --- whenever you can.

***As I wrote in Volume 1, "...words can make a difference." The words of a mother that I met (by chance) --- made a difference! The mother (in that story), lost her youngest child (to cancer); her kind words (to me) --- made me feel - 'beautiful inside.'

****Zeke did eventually get a dog (for a pet). When Zeke was 37 years old, his three (3) children gave him a dog (as a Father's Day present). Zeke's children wanted a dog and they were creative enough to know that Zeke would love their new pet (i.e., his Father's day puppy). Kids know how to get what they want. Zeke's dog was loved, but he had many health issues. He had Epilepsy and frequently had seizures; which shortened his life. He died at the age of nine.

*****Are there any 'chance encounters' in life or are all 'life events' --- part of: "Life's plan?" Continue reading; see what Zeke learns about Nature and people.

7.   Herman and Sherman

Herman and Sherman - unlikely friends they be ---
but both enjoyed each other's company.
They especially liked aiding - those in need ---
especially those who were --- being 'bullied.'
Read on and see - how Nature cares --- for 'Nature lovers.'

The next morning, Zeke and Billy were playing outside and they saw Uncle Eddie working in his garden. Billy said to Zeke, "Let's go over to Uncle Eddie's and see if he has any candy." Zeke responded, "Yeah, and I want to tell him how we were rescued from the Bullies."

As soon as they crossed the street, Billy asked Uncle Eddie if he had any candy. Then Zeke said, "Uncle Eddie, you won't believe what happened to Billy and me. Two squirrels and a hawk rescued us from the 'bully-boys.' Bruiser the Bully was going to take all of our candy, and a hawk swooped down and took his hat. Then two squirrels started throwing acorns at the Bullies. The bullies all ran away."

Uncle Eddie responded, "Wow! That's amazing, but I know about those animals. I know the names of those animals, too." Zeke responded, "What are their names?" Eddie then said to Zeke and Billy, "I'll bring out some lemonade and candy; while you're eating your candy I'll tell you about 'bullies' and those three animals."

While Zeke and Billy sat on Uncle Eddie's porch (drinking lemonade and eating candy), he told them about his childhood experience with 'Bullies.' Eddie told them that his Halloween candy was stolen, too. Zeke learned that 'teenage bullies' had stolen Eddie's bag of Halloween candy three (3) times - in one night.

The last time that Eddie went 'Trick-or-Treating' (as a child), teenagers stole his bag of candy; he went home crying and went out with another bag and the teenagers stole his second bag of candy. Eddie ran home crying and went out again to get Halloween candy, and the teenagers stole his third bag of candy. Eddie said that he cried all night and that he never went out 'Trick-or-Treating' again.

Zeke then said to Eddie, "That's horrible! I can't imagine having your candy being stolen three times in one night. My candy was stolen once, and I cried and cried. Is that why you like giving out candy to Billy and me?" Eddie responded, "Yes, I know how much joy a few pieces of candy can bring to children. I still love Halloween. I love to see all of the 'little kids' - dressed up in their favorite costumes. Halloween is a wonderful night --- if 'bullies' don't steal your candy."

Eddie then told Zeke and Billy, about children who were 'bullied' - when he was young. Zeke learned about Eddie's neighbor (a girl his age that was bullied). Zeke learned that there are 'girl bullies,' too. 'Bully-girls' made fun of Eddie's childhood friend. Mean-girls called Eddie's neighbor - 'mean' names; they made this girl's childhood very sad. Eddie said that his friend was tall, thin and attractive; but the 'bully girls' constantly were calling her 'mean names.' He said that his neighbor hated going to school or being with groups of girls - because they (girls in groups) always made fun of her.

Eddie told Zeke and Billy about the many types of people that are often 'bullied.' Eddie said, "Shy and timid kids are bullied, skinny kids too. Fat kids, short kids, handicapped kids, unathletic kids, kids with birthmarks, kids who stutter, kids who wear glasses, smart kids and kids who have problems learning (special needs kids) are often bullied."

Zeke and Billy learned that 'bullies' have been around forever. Eddie then told them about 'cyber-bullying.' Eddie said, "When I was young the 'bullies' would call you names or threaten to 'beat you up.' (punch you and kick you). Girl bullies would 'gossip' and write nasty things (on paper). Today, many kids are bullied on 'cell phones' or on social media sites. Kids don't write 'nasty notes' anymore; today they text 'nasty things' on their cell phones."

Zeke responded, "I don't have a cell phone;" Billy has one. I don't understand what you mean when you say: 'cyber-bullying.' I don't know what 'text' means or what 'social media' means."

Then Eddie said, "That's good that you don't text or use social media. When I was in school (long ago), the gym teacher would have boys who were mad at each other put on 'heavy boxing gloves.' If two boys wanted to fight or got mad (at each other), the gym teacher would say: 'Come to my office after school.' The gym teacher would put very heavy boxing gloves on the boys (who wanted to fight) and say: I'll let you swing at each other for 3 minutes. After about 30 seconds, the boys were exhausted and couldn't swing or punch each other (because the boxing gloves were so heavy). Then the gym teacher would talk to the boys (who were mad at each other). The boys would usually become friends after that.

But things are very different today. Today, gym teachers aren't allowed to let kids box - in school (to settle disagreements). Today, some kids who are bullied bring guns or weapons to school. And some kids, who are bullied, become loners; some even end their life. It's very sad for kids today, because kids today are always using their cell phones and they're always texting - often, texting 'nasty things' --- bullying! Zeke, I'm glad that you and Billy enjoy playing outside and exploring - in the woods and creeks; all kids should be outdoors and enjoying Nature --- like you two. <u>Nature never Bullies</u>; Nature just displays her beauty --- to all who look."

Zeke responded, "Uncle Eddie, you talk like Mr. Hill. I still don't understand what cyber-bullying or texting is, but I never write or say 'nasty things' --- about anyone. My dad told me: 'to treat everyone with respect;' to be 'polite' and always be nice."

Then Eddie said, "You both are very lucky; you both have good parents and they are showing you how to grow up. Not all children have good parents or grow-up in homes that have 'kind and loving parents.' Some children have parents that are mean; some children have dads that are mean - their dads make them into bullies. Some dads tell their sons to be 'rough and tough.' Bruiser's dad was like that. His dad made him become 'mean and tough,' and Bruiser is becoming like his dad - which is so sad."

Zeke then said to Eddie, "Uncle Eddie, you said you know the names of the squirrels and the hawk that rescued Billy and me; what are the names of those animals?" Eddie responded, "Long ago, when I was a little boy (like Billy and you), I had my Halloween candy stolen three (3) times - on Halloween night. The day after Halloween, I went down to the creek. I was very sad as I didn't have any Halloween candy to eat. Kids love to sort their Halloween candy and to arrange their Halloween candy. Having a big bag of Halloween candy is like a treasure trove.

As a child, I always enjoyed being outside and exploring in the woods. So the day after Halloween, I went down to the creek and sat on a log. I was feeling sad, and saw several turtles; they were sitting on logs on the other side of the creek. While I was sitting and looking at the turtles, a boy (around my age) walked up to me and asked me if I would like some of his Halloween cancy. I said: Thanks! I would love some candy. 'Mean' teenagers stole all of my Halloween candy last night. Teenagers stole my candy three times last night - I'm very sad because I don't have any Halloween candy. The boy looked at me and said, "That's horrible and sad. You can have my bag of candy; I have a lot more candy at home. It's wonderful to share things. My name is Herman, what's your name?"

As soon as Herman gave me his bag of Halloween candy, the 'Bully teenagers' came up to us. The one teenager (Bruiser's dad) said, 'Hey, little boy - give me your bag of candy!' As soon as he said that, 'little missiles' started hitting the 'mean' teenagers. Dozens of acorns were hitting the teenagers. The teenagers ran away from Herman and me. I looked up into the trees and I saw one squirrel throwing acorns at the mean teenagers and I saw another squirrel dropping dozens of acorns on the teenagers. Then I saw a 'Fish hawk' (an Osprey) fly over 'Bruiser the Bully' and drop a large fish on Bruiser's head. Herman and I couldn't believe it. We both said, 'Nature just rescued us from Bullies.' I then said to Herman, 'I'm going to call the one squirrel

Herman, because he saved your candy.' Herman responded, "Thanks Eddie, I like rhyming words. Does anyone in your family have a name that rhymes with Herman?"

I responded, "I have a cousin named Sherman. We can call the 'flying squirrel' Sherman. Herman and Sherman are words that rhyme. And we can call the Osprey - Ozzie, the Osprey. I like watching Ozzie and Harriet on TV." Herman responded, "I love to watch Ozzie and Harriet on TV, too."

Then Eddie said, "Herman and I became good friends. As children, we explored the woods and played in the creek. Our childhood was filled with adventures and fun outdoor activities. We would often see those two squirrels and occasionally see the Osprey. It seemed as if the Osprey and those two squirrels were constantly looking to protect 'Nature loving kids' from Bullies. Zeke, I think the squirrels that rescued you and Billy were taught by Herman and Sherman. Animals will teach their 'offspring' (their young) how to live; they teach them how to survive - it's called 'imprinting.' One day I'll tell you about 'animal imprinting.'

Zeke looked at Billy then said, "Uncle Eddie, I don't understand what 'imprinting' is but I like the names that you gave to the animals that rescued you - from the bullies. I'm going to call those animals by the same names. I know that those animals will take care of Billy and me. Mr. Hill said that I'm special and that Nature will show me its treasures. Now I know that Nature will also - Protect me --- from Bullies!"

****

*Halloween is a wonderful experience for children. Sadly, the writer did have his 'Trick-or-Treat' bag (of candy) stolen (3 times in one night) by teenagers (when he was a little boy). But the writer still loves to see and give candy to 'little ones' - on Halloween. The excitement and joy in 'little ones' - on Halloween is beautiful to see --- it never gets old. There is something magical, about seeing 'little ones' dressed up in their favorite costumes and then shouting (in their little voices) - 'Trick or Treat' --- on Halloween.

**Nature can and will rescue any and all people from sadness. If you are feeling sad or depressed, go out into Nature. Nature will always display its 'beauty' - to all; one but needs to spend time outdoors. John Burroughs said, "I go to nature to be soothed and healed, and to have my senses put in order."

***The Writer believes that 'Good Always overcomes Evil.' The writer also believes that it's important to: 'protect people' from 'Bullies.' Today, there are many ways to aid people - who are being 'bullied.' If you see someone being abused or bullied, please offer them assistance.

****Parents and caring adults (e.g., teachers, coaches, scout leaders, etc.) can instill or 'imprint' --- 'goodness.' Children can be taught how to be: 'kind & caring.' Children need 'Positive' Adult 'Role Models.'

*****Read on and see what Zeke discovers next.

8.   The 'S - O - S' in the Creek Water

The next morning, (after hearing Uncle Eddie's stories about 'Bullies'), Zeke's mind was 'racing;' Zeke's mind was often 'racing.' Zeke was always thinking about discovering treasures. Last night, Zeke had a dream about 'treasures.' In Zeke's dream, he learned that there were treasures - to be found in his 'hometown.'

After eating breakfast, Zeke decided that he wanted to go exploring and treasure hunting. Zeke decided to ask Billy if he wanted to go 'treasure hunting.' Before going to see Billy, Zeke thought about the treasures that he discovered on the barrier island beach - last summer. Zeke looked at his favorite treasures - his green sea glass, and his skeleton key. He also rubbed his fingers on his 'lucky charm' necklace (he wore his necklace every day). Zeke also took out the two notes that were given to him (the one note was from: 'the thing' - that lived under the jetty; the other note was from Mr. Hill). This made Zeke think of the 'special' adults that he met; Zeke thought of all of the adults that had told him that he was: 'special' and that he had a 'special gift.' Zeke's mind thought of: Mr. Hill, Mr. Ben, Nurse Coral, The fisherman with the featherless parakeet.

Then Zeke thought: 'Uncle Eddie' must be the next person who will help me discover treasures. Uncle Eddie must be an 'Omegan' - just like Mr. Hill. All of the 'special' people that Zeke met were - Nature lovers; they all are 'kind & caring people' who love Nature and they all like helping people who need help.

Zeke was excited. He couldn't wait to go exploring with Billy. Zeke was sure that his hometown had lots of treasures. Zeke knew that he was going to discover the treasures that existed in his little town.

After finishing breakfast, Zeke asked his mom if he could go exploring with Billy. Zeke's mom said, "Sure Zekie; just be home for lunch and don't catch any snakes. You know that I don't like snakes. Remember the time when the big Pine snake was in our yard and scared me. I called the police and the policeman came and shot the snake. Then he put the snake in the alley." Zeke responded, "I remember mom. We wouldn't go near the dead snake the rest of the day. Someone told us that snakes are still alive until it's nighttime. We believed that the dead snake could still bite us - even though the policeman killed it." Zeke's mom responded, "Zekie, that's a myth; it's not true. A dead snake is dead; it can't bite anyone after it's dead. Enjoy playing with Billy."

Zeke and Billy walked to the nearby creek. Zeke carried a bucket and Billy carried his net. Billy and Zeke planned on catching a turtle. Zeke was also hoping to discover a treasure. While walking to the creek, Zeke was fingering the 'green sea glass.' Zeke always carried his two treasures: 1) the skeleton key and 2) the green sea glass. Billy didn't know about Zeke's treasures. Billy just liked playing with Zeke. Billy and Zeke were becoming 'best friends.'

As soon as they got to the creek, Billy saw several turtles. Billy then said, "Zeke, remember my plan. You stay here and stare at the turtles; then I'll sneak around behind them and I'll catch one before it can jump back into the water." Zeke responded, "I remember; that's a great plan. I'll stay perfectly still and stare at the turtles."

While Billy was sneaking behind the turtles, Zeke noticed 'bubbles' - in the creek water. Zeke looked at the bubbles and he saw that there was a 'steady stream of bubbles.' Zeke kept staring at the bubbles and noticed that they were coming from the bottom of the creek. As Zeke stared at the bubbles (in the water), he saw an amazing sight. The bubbles (that had risen to the surface of the creek water), spelled: 'S-O-S.'

Zeke couldn't believe his eyes. Zeke's mind was thinking: "Nature needs my help. Nature is sending me a message." Zeke took out his 'green sea glass' and looked through it. Zeke's 'sea glass' magnified things. When Zeke looked through the sea glass, he saw a turtle on the bottom of the creek. The turtle was stuck on the bottom of the creek. Zeke instantly knew that the turtle needed to be rescued. The turtle was sending the 'S-O-S' message to Zeke.

As Zeke looked through his 'sea glass,' he noticed that it was a 'Box Turtle.' Box turtles don't swim or go into creeks; they're land turtles. Zeke instantly yelled to Billy, "Quick! Quick! Billy, come here quick! We have to rescue a turtle. There's a Box turtle stuck on the bottom of the creek. Hurry! Bring your net!"

Billy ran up to Zeke and dipped his net into the creek water. Billy scooped up the Box turtle (with his net). Billy quickly put his net on the ground. Zeke quickly lifted the Box turtle out of the net. Zeke and Billy couldn't believe their eyes. Someone had wrapped the Box turtle up in 'fishing string' and put heavy 'sinkers' (fishing weights) on the fishing line. Someone was trying to kill the Box turtle.

Zeke and Billy both said, "It must have been the mean teenagers that did this to the Box turtle. Some people are very mean. Why are some people so mean - to Nature?"

Zeke quickly removed the 'fishing string' from the Box turtle, but the turtle wasn't moving. The Box turtle was lying on the ground next to Zeke but not moving. It's head & neck were out of its shell, but it was motionless. Turtles always pull their head back into their shell when they see people. They think that people are predators (animals that want to eat them). Zeke felt sad for the turtle. Then Zeke thought - 'Zeke, you are special and have a gift --- Nature is counting on you to help it.'

Zeke's mind instantly 'flashed back' to the story of Marty and Murray. Zeke remembered how one muskrat rescued another; one muskrat did CPR on another and brought it back to life. Zeke said to Billy, "I'm going to save this turtle; I'm going to do

CPR on this turtle." Billy looked at Zeke and said, "You can't do CPR on a turtle; you can't push on its hard shell."

Zeke closed his eyes and took 3 deep breaths. When Zeke opened his eyes he said, "I have an idea. I'm going to push gently on the underbelly of the turtle and massage its neck at the same time."   Zeke was amazed at what he saw.

After a minute of massaging the turtle's neck, Zeke saw a 'little bit of water' trickle out of the turtle's mouth. Then the turtle tried to climb out of Zeke's hand. It was alive and scared; it wanted to run and hide.

Zeke quickly put the turtle down and it quickly went back into its shell. Billy instantly said, "Zeke, I can't believe what I just saw. You just saved a Box turtle. You are 'special' and have a special talent." Zeke responded, "Thanks for calling me special." Then Zeke looked closely at the motionless Box turtle. As Zeke looked at the turtle's shell, he noticed an unusual sight.   There was something different about the coloration of this turtle's shell.

Zeke then said, "Billy, look at this turtle's shell; it looks weird." Billy looked at the turtle's shell and said, "There's one patch on its shell that is different." Zeke then decided to take out his 'green sea glass' and look at the unusual coloring on the turtle's shell. Zeke was amazed at what he saw (when looking through the sea glass).

The one patch on the turtle's shell looked like a 'store barcode.' It looked like the square designs (matrix codes) that stores put on individual items. People can take cell phone pictures of barcodes and pay for those items with their cell phones. Zeke also noticed that there were numbers under the 'barcode like patch.' Zeke saw the numbers: (1,1,2,3.5...and 3,4,5 with a triangle picture). Zeke instantly thought: 'Fibonacci sequence;' this has to be a treasure. Zeke knew that he had discovered his first treasure - in his hometown. Now, Zeke was sure that there were more treasures in his hometown.

Zeke's mind was 'racing' and thinking of treasures and what this code must mean. Then Zeke said; "Billy, take a picture of the turtle's shell. Take a picture of the shell with your cell phone." After Billy took a picture of the turtle's shell, they decided to bring the turtle to Uncle Eddie.

Zeke knew that Mr. Hill would be able to tell him what the 'design or unusual pattern' (that was on the turtle's shell), meant. Zeke was sure that this was a treasure. But Zeke knew that he wouldn't be able to see Mr. Hill for a long time. Zeke's dad wouldn't be going to the barrier island beach again, until next summer --- next summer was 9 months from now.

Zeke was sure that Uncle Eddie would help him! Zeke believed that Uncle Eddie was 'special' and that he had a 'gift' - like Mr. Hill. Zeke knew that Uncle Eddie was an 'Omegan' - a Nature lover & Nature aider. Uncle Eddie knew a lot about Nature and he talked like Mr. Hill (i.e., he used words that little Zeke didn't understand). Uncle Eddie was: 'a kind and caring' adult who loved Nature. Zeke was sure that Uncle Eddie would explain what the 'barcode' (on the turtle's shell) meant.

While walking home with the Box turtle, Zeke told Billy about Mr. Hill and how special he was. Then Zeke said, "Billy, I think Uncle Eddie is 'special' - like Mr. Hill." Billy responded, "I don't know Mr. Hill. but Uncle Eddie knows a lot about Nature and Gardening; I'm sure that he'll know why this turtle's shell has that weird design. And we can eat some of Uncle Eddie's candy while he's looking at our turtle. Uncle Eddie always has candy and he likes to share it with us."

As they were walking to Uncle Eddie's house, Zeke and Billy were talking about keeping the Box turtle as a pet. They were planning on building a 'turtle pen' and feeding their 'Box turtle' pet earthworms and vegetables. Zeke and Billy knew that turtles eat worms and they knew that Uncle Eddie raised earthworms - he had an outdoor compost bin that had thousands of earthworms. Zeke and Billy also knew that Uncle Eddie would give them earthworms to feed to their new pet - their 'special Box turtle.'

When they got back to Billy's house, Zeke saw Uncle Eddie working in his garden. Zeke yelled, "Uncle Eddie, Billy and I just caught a Box turtle and it has 'weird' markings on its shell. I know that Mr. Hill would know what those markings mean but he lives far away. Uncle Eddie, you are 'special' (like Mr. Hill); will you look at our turtle and tell us what those markings mean?" Uncle Eddie responded, "Let me see your turtle."

Zeke and Billy ran across the street to Uncle Eddie's. As soon as Eddie looked at the Box turtle's shell, he said: "WOW! Boys, I've seen lots of Box turtles but I have never seen 'markings' like that on any turtle." Then Eddie said, "Those markings do look like a: 'store's barcode design.' Then Eddie said, "I'm going to take a picture of this turtle's shell and send the picture to my nephew." My nephew has a friend who is an 'animal expert.' My nephew's friend is a professor and a Biologist. My nephew will be able to find out what these markings mean."

Then Eddie proceeded to tell Zeke & Billy about technology. Eddie said, "When I was little, cellphones didn't exist. Today, technology helps people learn new things. Technology is constantly changing. The picture that I just took (of your turtle) will get to my nephew - in a few seconds." Zeke responded, "How can that be? I see the picture on your phone; how can it get from your phone to your nephew? Is this a magic trick or are you just trying to 'trick' me and Billy?"

Eddie began telling Zeke and Billy about 'satellites' orbiting the Earth and how people can send texts and 'Email' messages around the world - in a few seconds. Zeke couldn't believe it. Zeke couldn't believe that people could use a cellphone to 'navigate' - when they are driving in their car. Zeke was amazed, as he listened to Uncle Eddie talk about technology and what it could do.

As Eddie continued to talk about technology, he said: "Technology is a great thing when it is used to learn or help people. But technology can be a bad thing. <u>Good people</u> are using technology to aid & help Nature --- they are using it to learn how to sustain Nature; much of our Natural world is threatened." Then Eddie said, "<u>Bad people</u> are using technology - to do bad things. 'Bullies' use technology to 'bully' and spread lies.' Be careful with technology --- NEVER Cyber-Bully!"

Zeke then said, "Uncle Eddie, you talk like Mr. Hill. You use words that I don't understand. Mr. Hill would often talk to me using words that I didn't understand. Mr. Hill is 'special' - like you. Do you know Mr. Hill?"

Eddie responded, "No, I don't know Mr. Hill. But when I look at your turtle's shell I see Fibonacci's sequence. Then Eddie said, "1,1,2,3,5 ...Trust, Believe and Receive." Zeke instantly responded, "Mr. Hill said those same words to me. He said that his father and his father's real estate friend would sit on his porch and they used those words. They (Mr. Hill's dad and Seppie) would often say, "Trust your gut, believe in yourself and you will receive what you need --- you will always get what is needed to get through any difficult event or day." Then Zeke took out his 'green sea glass' and said, "Uncle Eddie, this is one of my treasures - it has the letters T,B,R on it and the numbers 1,1,2,3. It's one of my treasures and it magnifies things.   Uncle Eddie, do you know a man named Seppie? Seppie sold Mr. Hill's dad the house that he lives in and he had an unusual pet. Seppie's pet rabbit smelled like lavender."

Eddie responded, "I don't know Mr. Hill, but I heard about a real estate man who had an unusual pet rabbit. The real estate man's name was Giuseppe. He was Italian and came to America long ago. Giuseppe left Italy long ago and brought his pet rabbit with him. Giuseppe kept the rabbit in his suitcase, when he immigrated from Italy to the United States. There were many stories told about Giuseppe and his pet rabbit. Giuseppe and people like him (Italians) were not liked in this town. Italians were considered an 'invasive species.' This town originally was a 'German settlement.' One day I will tell you about 'invasive species' and Italian immigrants in this town.

Little Zeke, your dad is Italian, his father came here from Italy. Your dad is lucky that Mr. Henry is his neighbor. Mr. Henry's family is one of the original German families that settled into this town long ago. Mr. Henry is 'nice & kind' to everyone in his neighborhood. Mr. Henry is the perfect neighbor. He and your dad are good friends. Long ago, your grandfather and other Italians were called 'mean & nasty' names; people called them 'WOPS.' The word 'wop' meant: <u>without papers</u> - meaning that Italians shouldn't be here; meaning that they came to America illegally. Your Dad's parents came here legally; but they and other Italians were treated unfairly.   If you weren't a German, you and your family would be 'harassed and treated unfairly;' you would also be called 'derogatory' names."

Zeke responded, "Uncle Eddie, I don't understand what invasive species means or what immigrant means or what 'without papers' means, but I have two 'special papers;' they are notes that were given to me. I think of them as treasures. Mr. Hill gave me the one paper (note) and 'a thing' gave me the other paper (note). The thing lived under the jetty. I don't have those papers (notes) with me but one day I will let you read them.   Mr. Hill told me to only show them to people who were 'Omegans;' he said that only Omegans would believe what they say. Uncle Eddie, are you an Omegan?"

Eddie responded, "Yes, I am! And I live by the Indian proverb: 'We don't inherit the land from our ancestors, we borrow it from our children.' Little Zeke, let me see your 'green sea glass'. I like sea glass and have some; one day I'll show you and Billy my sea glass collection."

Zeke took his green sea glass out of his pocket and handed it to Eddie. Eddie looked through the 'green sea glass' and said, "Wow! This is special; it's a magnifier!" Then Eddie held the green sea glass over the Box turtle's shell and said, "There are numbers under the 'barcode' design. I see Fibonacci's sequence and then there are the numbers: 3,4,5 and a triangle shape."

Zeke responded, "That has to be a 'special code;' those numbers will lead me to another treasure. The Fibonacci numbers led me to the treasure on the jetty. I know those numbers mean something. Uncle Eddie what do those numbers mean?"

Eddie responded, "Since there is a triangle design next to the numbers: (3,4,5), I think they are referring to a 'right triangle.' Maybe there is a right triangle in the woods that has a treasure inside of it. But the numbers may also stand for words. Zeke, you are 'special' and Nature is leading you to its many treasures. I'm sure that Nature will lead you to another treasure.

Zeke, there was another 'special' man who had a special code number. That man's name was Mr. Rogers and his special number was: 143. The number 143 meant: 'I love you.' Maybe the numbers 345 on the turtle's shell refer to a 'special set of words.' Think of a word phrase with the first word having 3 letters, the second word having 4 letters and the third word having 5 letters."

Zeke knew that the Box turtle, that he rescued from the creek, would lead him to another treasure. Zeke's mind was 'racing' and thinking about discovering more treasures, but Zeke was clueless; he had no idea what the number 345 could mean or what a right triangle was. Zeke just knew that he was 'special' and that Nature would lead him to its treasures. Zeke also now knew that there was another 'special' adult - in his life. Zeke now knew that Uncle Eddie was an Omegan. Uncle Eddie was 'special;' just like Mr. Hill, Mr. Ben, and Nurse Coral.

Then Zeke said, "Uncle Eddie, I don't understand a lot of the things that you talked about, and I don't know Mr. Rogers. But I will try to think of a word phrase that the number 345 could mean. I know that Nature will lead me to another treasure and I'm very happy that you are an 'Omegan.' You are very 'kind & nice' - just like Mr. Hill and Mr. Ben. Can Billy and I have a few pieces of candy, before we leave? We're going to go build a turtle pen for our turtle. We're going to keep the Box turtle as our pet.

Eddie responded, "Sure you can have some candy, but I think that you should return the Box turtle to its natural habitat. You should take the turtle back to the woods. That Box turtle is a beautiful piece of Nature, but Nature doesn't want it to be a pet. It has a role to play in its Natural habitat. It is wonderful that you rescued and aided Nature. I'm glad that you and Billy enjoy exploring and spending time in the nearby creeks and woods. One day I'll tell you about the 'special water,' that's in the creek. Enjoy your turtle today, but return it to the woods tomorrow."

Zeke looked at Eddie, then said: "You're right Uncle Eddie, the turtle should be living in the woods with its turtle family. It probably misses its turtle cousins. Billy and I will take the Box turtle back to the woods now and we'll eat some of your candy as we walk back to the creek. Thanks, for talking to us and for the candy. You're really nice and know a lot about Nature --- you're a lot like Mr. Hill."

Eddie looked at Zeke and said, "Thanks for calling me: 'nice.' Come and see me anytime, and I will gladly answer any questions that you have about Nature or Gardening. Keep exploring and enjoying Nature! I'll let you know what my nephew says, when he sees the picture of your Box turtle's shell."

Zeke responded, "Bye Uncle Eddie! Thanks again for the candy and talking to us. We're going to give our Box turtle a name - before we release it; we're going to call it 'Earl.' It's a regal and noble turtle; Earls are nobles and famous in England."

****

9. The Special Mud

When Zeke and Billy got back to the creek (with their Box Turtle), they took the turtle out of the bucket and put it on the ground. Zeke decided to watch the turtle; he wanted to see where the turtle would go. When Zeke put the turtle down he said, "Little Earl, you are free. We rescued you from the 'mean teenagers.' Now you are free to live as a beautiful Box turtle. I know that you will lead me to another treasure. Little Earl, show me where the next treasure is."

Zeke and Billy decided to watch and follow the turtle as it began to walk away. The turtle walked into the woods. The turtle walked under some briars (sticker bushes), as it walked deeper into the woods. Billy said to Zeke, "Zeke, I'm not going to get cut up by the briars; they make me bleed. You can follow the turtle, I'll wait here." Zeke responded, "Briars do hurt, but I want to see where Earl (our turtle) is going to go; I'll be careful. I'll be back in a few minutes."

Zeke climbed through the briar patch (sticker bushes), and did get cut. Zeke had scratches and cuts on his hands, arms and his legs (from the thorns on the briars), but Zeke was sure that the turtle would lead him to another treasure. Within a few minutes, Zeke saw the turtle walking into a mud puddle. Zeke noticed that the Box turtle was stuck; it couldn't get out of the mud. Zeke bent down and lifted the turtle out of the mud and placed the turtle safely on the dry ground. Then Zeke said, "Little turtle, this is the second time that I had to rescue you. I didn't think that you would get stuck in the mud, but you did." As soon as Zeke said this to the turtle, the turtle looked at Zeke. Then the turtle turned and looked at the mud. The turtle looked at the mud again, then looked up at Zeke; it did that three (3) times.

Before the turtle continued to walk into the woods, it looked at Zeke and it did the most unusual thing; it 'smiled, winked and nodded' at Zeke. Zeke couldn't believe what he saw. Then Zeke's mind thought: "Zeke, you are special. Nature knows that you are special. Nature needs and wants your help. This turtle is part of Nature and it is telling you - 'Thanks for rescuing me.' This turtle also looked at the mud, then looked at you. The turtle is telling you that there's a treasure in that mud puddle."

Zeke looked at the turtle one last time and said, "Thanks Earl, for showing me where the next treasure is." Earl (the turtle), looked at Zeke and smiled, winked and nodded. Zeke smiled, winked and nodded back at the turtle; then the turtle turned and walked away from Zeke.

Zeke knelt down by the 'mud puddle' and sifted through the mud. Zeke thought that he would find some buried treasure in the mud. Zeke was sure that there was something buried under the mud. Zeke used his hands to 'scoop up' mud, but he didn't find anything buried in the mud. Even though Zeke didn't find any treasures (buried in the mud), he did make a few 'mud pies.' All kids love to make 'mud pies.'

While kneeling by the mud puddle (that was in the woods), Zeke watched the turtle walk deeper into the woods. Then Zeke decided to go back to Billy and show him the 'mud pies,' that he made. When Billy saw Zeke he said, "Zeke, you're all cut-up and scratched. Your arms and legs are bleeding and cut. That's why I didn't want to go through the briar patch. We better get you home so that your mom can clean up your cuts." Zeke then said, "Billy, Earl got stuck in a mud puddle and I had to rescue him, again. The turtle told me that the mud puddle had a treasure in it. I didn't find the treasure, but I made some beautiful mud pies; Billy, look at my mud pies."

Zeke took one 'mud pie' out of his pocket and handed it to Billy. Billy looked at the mud pie and said, "Wow! Great mud pie." Then Billy said, "This mud is warm. My hand feels warm and tingly, when I hold this mud pie." Then Billy gave the mud pie back to Zeke.

Zeke thanked Billy for saying that he made a 'great mud pie.' Zeke's mind was racing and thinking about what Billy had just said. When Billy said that Zeke's mud pie made his hand feel 'warm & tingly,' Zeke thought of Mr. Ben's 'healing pearls.' Zeke remembered how 'the healing pearls' would make his hands 'warm and tingly.' Zeke's mind was thinking: maybe this is 'special mud' - maybe it's 'healing mud.'

Zeke and Billy walked back to Zeke's house. As soon as Zeke's mom saw him she said, "Zekie, you're a mess! How did you get so muddy? Come around to the back door and take off all of your clothes in the laundry room. I don't want all of that mud tracked into the house."

Billy knew that Zeke's mom would need a lot of time to tend to Zeke's cuts and scratches, so he told Zeke that he would play with him tomorrow. Zeke's mom told Zeke to go into the bathroom and wash his hands, arms & legs with soap and water. Zeke knew that his mom was going to put medicine on his cuts and scratches. Zeke didn't want his mom to put any alcohol or Iodine on his cuts and scratches. Iodine and Alcohol burn, when you put it on cuts and scratches.

Zeke was amazed at what he saw when he rinsed the mud off of his 'cut-up' hands. When Zeke looked at his clean hands, the cuts and scratches were --- all gone. There weren't any cuts or scratches on his hands. Zeke's legs and arms had lots of cuts and scratches (from the briar patch thorns), but the cuts & scratches on Zeke's hands were gone; they were healed.

Zeke's mind instantly thought: "The mud is special; it's healing mud." Then Zeke heard his mom say, "Zeke, I'm going to put some medicine on your cuts so that they don't get infected." Zeke instantly said, "Mom! I don't need any medicine; the mud healed the cuts on my hands. Alcohol and Iodine burn; don't put them on my cuts. Please Mom! No Iodine; I'm fine."

Zeke didn't convince his mother. Zeke's mom still put Iodine on all of Zeke's scratches. Zeke screamed: "OUCH!' - as his mother applied Iodine to his cuts and scratches. Iodine and Alcohol burn when they are put on to cuts and scratches, but Zeke always did what his mother said.

When Zeke went to bed that night he kept thinking about: 'Special mud' and 'healing pearls.' Zeke was convinced that the mud was 'special.' Zeke knew that he had found another treasure. Zeke knew that Earl (the Box turtle) had led him to the 'special mud puddle.' Before falling asleep, Zeke thought about his two 'mud pies.' His two mud pies were still in his pants pocket. Zeke knew that his mom would throw them out; so Zeke quietly walked down stairs into the laundry room and got the two mud pies out of his pants. Zeke put his 'special mud pies' into a plastic bag and brought them up into his bedroom. Zeke decided to try an experiment with his mud pies. But Zeke's experiment would have to wait until tomorrow.

It was late and Zeke was tired. Zeke smiled as he laid in his bed. Little Zeke was happy; he had another wonderful day. Every day that a person gets to play outside in the woods is a great day. Every day that a person gets to play with their 'best friend' is a great day. When a person gets to go exploring (in the woods) with their best friend, it's a great day! Today, Zeke discovered a 'treasure,' while exploring with his best friend - so it was: a SUPER GREAT DAY! But before Zeke fell asleep he heard his older brother (Zack) yell upstairs to him. Zack was yelling: "Zeke! Did the monsters get you? Zeke, answer me! Did the Monsters eat you?" Zeke didn't answer, as he quickly fell asleep; Zeke was dreaming about going exploring with his best friend (Billy). Zeke was dreaming about all of the treasures that he would find in his hometown. Zeke's mind kept repeating: "Zeke, you are special; you have a gift --- Nature will lead you to its treasures."

Zeke never told Zack that he discovered - that there aren't any monsters living under Zeke's bed. Zack still believes that there are monsters living under the beds and in the attic of the house that he and Zeke grew up in. Some people learn and outgrow their childhood fears; Zeke did --- Omegans know this; but Alpha's like Zack don't.

Some people remain 'fearful;' like Zack. Nature can teach everyone how to live and how to overcome fears.

****

10. The Special Water

When Zeke got up the next morning, he wanted to try an experiment with his mud pies. Zeke was convinced that his 'mud pies' had special healing powers. Zeke believed that the mud healed the cuts on his hands. Zeke's hands were cut and scratched by the briar thorns yesterday. But all of the cuts on Zeke's hands had healed.

Zeke was going to rub some mud on his leg cuts. He wanted to see if the mud would heal the scratches & cuts that were on his legs . Zeke's experiment would have to wait. Billy was knocking on Zeke's door. Zeke put one mud pie into his pants pocket and ran down stairs and opened the door for Billy.

Billy was wearing his baseball glove and wanted to play catch with Zeke. Zeke told Billy, "My glove is upstairs. I'll go get it." Zeke ran upstairs and put his mud pie back into his dresser drawer, then ran downstairs with his baseball glove. Zeke told his mother that he would be outside playing catch with Billy. Zeke's mom said, "Have fun boys!"

Billy said to Zeke, "Zeke, you be the pitcher and I'll be the catcher. I'll make a home plate on the sidewalk with my chalk. I'll call 'balls & strikes.' Let's see how many 'strike outs' you can get and how many 'walks' you give up." Zeke responded, "OK Billy, I love to pitch and you are a good catcher."

Billy made a home plate on the sidewalk (with his chalk), then he and Zeke began playing 'pitch and catch.' They pretended that they were 'battery mates' (pitcher and catcher). They pretended that they were playing an 'imaginary game' of baseball. They wanted to see if Zeke could pitch a 'perfect game' --- a 'no hitter!'

After Zeke threw Billy a few 'warm-up' pitches, Billy said, "OK Zeke, let's get the first batter out. I'll give you the 'sign' (#1 means: fastball, #2 means: curveball, #3 means: knuckleball). Zeke responded, "OK Billy, I'm ready; give me the sign for the pitch you want me to throw." Billy squatted down and gave Zeke the #1 sign. Zeke wound up and threw the ball to Billy. Billy caught the ball and yelled: "Strike one!" Then Billy gave Zeke the sign for the next pitch. Billy put down two fingers; he gave Zeke the #2 (the sign for a curve ball). Zeke put his fingers in his back pocket then gripped the baseball. Zeke wound up and threw the ball to Billy. Billy caught the ball then said, "Strike two! Great pitch Zeke; that pitch had 'great movement' - it dropped and curved! I've never seen you throw a pitch like that and it was right at the knees --- perfect location!"

Billy looked at the 'imaginary batter' then gave Zeke the next sign; he showed Zeke the #1 sign --- Billy wanted Zeke to throw him a 'fastball.' Zeke wound up and threw the ball to Billy. Billy caught the ball and said, "Strike three! Batter, you're out!" Then Billy looked at Zeke and said, "Zeke, that ball really moved. I gave you the sign for a fastball but you threw me a knuckleball. That pitch had a lot of movement."

Zeke responded, "I didn't throw you a knuckleball. My pitches just have a lot of movement today. I don't know why my pitches are moving so much today. The ball feels alive; I feel like I'm Whitey Ford, or Warren Spahn or Sandy Koufax. This is a lot of fun. I've got control of all of my pitches today." Billy responded, "I've never seen your pitches move that much or your fastball go that fast. Did you have Wheaties (the breakfast of champions) for breakfast this morning?" Zeke responded, "I had Frosted Flakes for breakfast this morning. I like Frosted Flakes better than Wheaties but I do eat Wheaties sometimes."

Zeke thought about what Billy had just said: "...that Zeke's pitches were great today; that his pitches had 'great movement' and that he had great control today." Then Zeke looked at his hands. When Zeke looked at his fingers he saw mud on his fingers and mud underneath his fingernails. Zeke instantly thought: "The mud is special. Not only is it 'healing mud' but it also gives my fingers 'special powers;' it enables me to be a great baseball pitcher."

Zeke and Billy decided to take a break. They saw Uncle Eddie working in his garden. Eddie was putting leaves and food scraps into his compost pile. Billy looked at Zeke and said, "Let's go get some candy from Uncle Eddie." Zeke responded, "Yeah! And I want to tell him that we took the Box turtle back to the woods."

As soon as they crossed the street, Billy yelled: "Uncle Eddie, do you have any candy?" Eddie responded, "Let me put the lid back on my compost bin, then I'll bring some candy out for the two of you."

Eddie covered his 'compost bin' and handed a bowl of candy to Billy. He told Zeke and Billy to take a few pieces of candy from the bowl. As Billy was picking out candy, Zeke said to Eddie, "Uncle Eddie we took the Box turtle back to the woods and let it go. I followed it and it got stuck in a 'mud puddle.' I had to rescue it again. It couldn't get out of the mud puddle. I got cut-up and scratched by briars, look at all of the scratches on my legs and arms."

Eddie looked at Zeke's legs and arms and said, "Wow! You have a lot of scratches. Briars hurt; they have lots of thorns. I see that your mom put Iodine on your cuts." Zeke then said, "I don't like Iodine; it burns. My mom always puts Iodine on my cuts. She didn't put any Iodine on my hands because the cuts on my hands were healed by the mud.

The mud puddle that the Box turtle was stuck in had special mud. I made a few 'mud pies.' And the mud healed all of the cuts on my hands. The mud is special just like the 'healing pearls' that Mr. Ben makes necklaces from. Mr. Ben makes special healing necklaces from pearls. I think the 'healing pearls' are growing in 'special water.' I think that the mud puddle that the turtle was stuck in has 'special water.' I think that the water made the mud special; my mud pies made my hands feel 'warm & tingly.' Uncle Eddie do you think that my mud pies could have been in 'special water?' The Box turtle kept looking at the mud puddle; it kept pointing to the mud puddle. I know that the turtle was telling me that there was a treasure in that mud puddle. Nature always leads me to its treasures. Mr. Hill told me that I'm special and that Nature will show me all of its treasures."

Before Eddie could respond, Billy said to Zeke: "Zeke, let me see your hands. Show me your fingers." Zeke held out his hands and Billy said: "Zeke, your fingers are muddy. You 'doctored' your pitches. That's why your pitches were moving so much. You were throwing 'mud ball' pitches to me. That is special mud. You never were able to pitch like that; your pitches today were --- unbelievable!"

Eddie then responded, "Boys, do you know that Major League baseballs are 'rubbed down' with special mud? All Major League baseballs are 'polished and rubbed' with 'special mud.' The location of the 'special mud' is a secret, but I know that the special mud that is used on Major League baseball comes from a place near here. The exact location is kept a secret."

Then Eddie looked at Zeke and said, "Zeke, your question about special water is interesting. Long ago, people traveled to our town to wade in the creek that you rescued the Box turtle from. People believed that the water in our creeks had 'special healing powers.' People came from far away; many traveled long distances just to wade in our creek. They would wade in our creek or sit in it. They believed that it could cure a variety of illnesses. Maybe the water is special. We call our creek water - 'Cedar Water' because of its Amber & Orange color and the fact that our creeks flow through groves of Cedar trees.

Zeke, what I know is that Nature has the answer to everything. Nature knows how to adapt and change. It will cure itself; it will adapt and heal from all of the horrible things that humans do to it. Many of the medicines that we use today came from Nature. Scientists are continuing to learn 'new things' from Nature. Scientists are creating new medicines everyday. Scientists know that Nature has the answers to every human problem. There are still many mysteries. There are mysteries in Nature that remain unsolved and there are family mysteries.

Little Zeke, I'm sure of one thing; whenever I'm outdoors and enjoying Nature I feel better! Keep enjoying Nature. Keep exploring and learning from Nature. And Keep having fun playing baseball; but don't 'doctor' the baseball."

Zeke looked at Uncle Eddie and said, "I didn't know that Major League baseballs were 'polished and rubbed' with special mud. I will always be kind to Nature and will always help it survive. I wasn't trying to 'doctor' the baseball when I threw it. I think - the mud made my fingers have 'special powers.' Thanks for telling Billy and me about the special creek water and thanks for sharing your candy with us. You are always - nice and very kind."

Eddie looked at Zeke and said, "Any time that you have questions about Nature or Gardening - ask me. I will always be here to answer your questions. There are many 'unique things' - about this town; I will gladly tell you what I know about this town. Keep enjoying playing outdoors! You and Billy are good friends and I enjoy seeing you two, especially when you are playing baseball. Keep having fun!"

****

*Earth is called the 'Water Planet;' most of our planet is water. But most of the water on Earth is salt water; it can't be used by humans. Most of the Earth's water is in the oceans & seas; it's too saline (salty) - so humans can't drink it. It is imperative for humans to keep our creeks, streams, rivers and groundwater clean. All rivers flow to the ocean. The oceans are threatened by human trash and pollution that flows from rivers into the ocean. Remember and live by the Indian phrase: "We don't inherit the land from our ancestors, we borrow it from our children." Help keep our 'waterways' clean! Don't use pesticides or over fertilize your lawn. Algae blooms are often caused by fertilizer runoff; they kill fish and affect the ocean's ecosystem.
**MLB baseballs are 'rubbed' with special mud.

11. Adaptations

After visiting Uncle Eddie and hearing him talk about the town's creeks having special water, Zeke knew that his mud was special. Zeke believed that his mud had 'special powers.' Tonight, when Zeke hopped into bed he planned on dreaming about his next treasure. But before Zeke could think or dream about treasures, he had to listen to his older brother. As soon as Zeke got into his bed, Zack yelled: "Zeke! Did the monsters get you? Did the monsters eat you? Answer me!" Zeke did answer Zack; he said: "No Zack, the monsters didn't get me. The monsters are waiting for you because they know that you are afraid of them!"

Zeke knew that his town had treasures. Zeke had discovered two (2) treasures (in his hometown): 1) the Box turtle with the 'barcode design,' and 2) the mud pies; but Zeke was clueless. Zeke had no idea what the 'barcode' design meant. Zeke also had no idea what the numbers 3,4,5 could mean or what three word phrase they could stand for. Zeke knew and believed that Nature would lead him to all of its treasures and he now knew that his hometown had lots of treasures. Zeke also knew and believed that Nature would protect him from 'Bullies.' Zeke was asleep within two minutes.

Little Zeke slept well that night! Children always sleep well after playing outside all day. When Zeke awoke the next morning, he remembered words from his dream. The words: "You will learn" and "You will teach," kept running through Zeke's mind. Zeke knew that he had heard them before, but he couldn't remember who had said them.

Zeke's mind was 'racing' again; his mind was often racing. He decided to eat breakfast then go play catch with Billy. When Zeke was approaching Billy's house he saw Uncle Eddie outside. Eddie was working in his garden. Zeke yelled to Eddie, he said: "Uncle Eddie, did you tell me the words 'you will learn' or the words 'you will teach?' I had a dream and I know that someone said those words to me."

Eddie responded, "No Zeke, I didn't. But remember, I told you to think of a three word phrase. Remember how I told you that Mr. Rogers had a special number phrase; his code was 143 and it meant 'I love you.' Mr. Rogers spent his adult life teaching people how to be kind. He lived by the phrase: '<u>kindness is love in action</u>.' Maybe (you will teach), is your special phrase. What were the code numbers - that were on the turtle's shell?"

Zeke responded, "The numbers (on the turtle's shell) were 345." Eddie responded, "They could be your special phrase. You (has 3 letters), will (has 4 letters) and learn & teach (each have 5 letters). Maybe you are supposed to become a teacher."

Zeke instantly remembered Mr. Hill saying: "Zeke, you are special. You have gifts and Nature will lead you to all of its treasures. Nature is counting on you to aid it and help it survive. Zeke, you will teach others how to treat Nature and how to help it survive."

Then Zeke said, "Uncle Eddie, Mr. Hill told me that I would teach. Mr. Hill said that I had a gift and one of my gifts was that I am a great teacher. I told Mr. Hill that I am very shy and that I would never be able to talk to people and teach anyone. Mr. Hill said that 'example' - is the best teacher. He said that people will learn from me just by watching how I treat others and how I treat Nature."

Eddie responded, "Mr. Hill is correct. <u>Example is the best teacher</u>. People will learn how to treat others and how to treat Nature - by watching you. Zeke, you are very kind and you are nice to Nature. We are all students and we are all teachers. There are many things that Nature will teach us. We all can learn from Nature and then we can use what Nature teaches us to make our lives better. Nature has all of the answers. Nature is constantly adapting and changing. If Nature doesn't adapt, it won't survive. The Dinosaurs didn't adapt and they became extinct. Zeke, you do have a unique & special connection to Nature. You can 'see' - beauty in the tiniest of things.

You can see Nature's beauty - even with your eyes closed; you are 'blessed.' Think about this: 'Is a dead tree really dead' or is it another life form?"

Zeke responded, "Of course a dead tree is dead. That's a silly question or a trick question. Eddie then said, "Zeke, the next time that you are in the woods find a dead tree. Find a tree that doesn't have any leaves growing from its branches, then look carefully at the dead tree and tell me what you see. " Zeke responded, "OK, but I know that you are trying to trick me."

Eddie then talked to Zeke about the many ways that Nature adapts to sudden changes. Zeke learned about 'invasive species.' Eddie told Zeke how people brought Gypsy Moths to the United States from Europe. Scientists wanted the moths to make silk. The Gypsy moth caterpillars got out of the Scientists laboratory and ate the leaves off of many forest trees. The Gypsy moths are just one example of humans creating problems for Nature.

Eddie told Zeke that Nature now has to adapt to 'Climate Change.' The Earth's climate is changing. Humans are making it worse. Some 'rich & powerful' humans deny that the Earth's climate is changing. Most scientists believe that humans are a major cause of climate change and that humans can aid Nature. Zeke then said, "I aid Nature. I help Nature and people whenever I can. Does that mean that I'm adapting? Does that mean that I won't go extinct?"

Eddie laughed at Zeke's comment about becoming extinct, then said: "A great scientist named Charles Darwin said: 'It's not the strongest that survive; it's the ones who are the most adaptable to change.' Humans need to adapt, too. Many humans are adapting. Remember how I told you about the Gypsy moth being an 'invasive species' that destroyed many forests. I also told you that (long ago) the leaders of this town looked at your family as an 'invasive species.' Long ago, this town was a German settlement. The townspeople looked at other ethnic groups as 'invasive species.' The townspeople only wanted Germanic people living here. This town adapted. This town has people from many different ethnicities. Our town is a wonderful town thanks to people like Mr. Henry.

Mr. Henry is - 'the Perfect Neighbor.' Mr. Henry has befriended and aided many people in this neighborhood. Mr. Henry is nice to everyone. He doesn't care if you are an Italian, or if you are Irish, Hispanic, African American, Jewish, Protestant or Catholic; he's nice and helpful to everyone in his neighborhood. Mr. Henry is one example of people adapting and changing. One day I will tell you more about Mr. Henry. I also will tell you about people overcoming and adapting to missing legs and arms. There are many handicapped people who have adapted to their handicaps and they are productive in their communities. There are also handicapped animals that are surviving - thanks to caring humans. One day I will tell you about my friend's 3-legged cat."

Zeke was an intent listener, and he was enjoying Uncle Eddie's stories. Then Zeke heard his friend Billy yell, "Uncle Eddie, do you have any candy?" Eddie responded, "Sure Billy. Come over." Then he said to Zeke: "Remember that Nature is showing people how to live, and adapt to change. Let Nature teach you, then you will teach others how to live and be - 'one with Nature.' Little Zeke, you truly are special and you have a unique connection to Nature."

Zeke responded to Eddie by saying: "Thanks for talking to me and telling me about Nature and our town. And thanks for calling me special. Uncle Eddie, you really are 'special & nice;' you're a lot like Mr. Hill."

****

*Communities that adapt and are accepting of various ethnic groups tend to be thriving communities. Our world is better when neighborhoods have neighbors like Mr. Henry. Mr. Henry truly was kind and helpful to everyone!
**James Barrie said, "Those who bring sunshine into the lives of others cannot keep it from themselves." Mr. Henry brought lots of sunshine into his community.
***R.L. Stevenson said: "Don't judge each day by the harvest that you reap but by the seeds that you plant." To that I would add: "If you sow the seeds of 'kindness,' you will reap an abundant crop of joy."
****Nature truly has all of the answers and teaches all who go to her. Emerson said: "Adopt the pace of Nature, her secret is patience." John Muir said: "The clearest way into the universe is through a forest wilderness." Aristotle said: "In all things of Nature, there is something marvelous." And Shakespeare said: "One touch of Nature makes the whole world kin." I agree!

12. Invasive Species

After listening to Uncle Eddie talking to him about Adaptations and Nature, Zeke knew that Nature was going to teach him many new things. Zeke also knew that Nature was going to lead him to its treasures. Zeke believed that the numbers: 3,4,5 were special numbers. He believed that they meant: "You will learn and You will teach."

Zeke was excited about learning all of the things that Nature could teach him, but Zeke didn't believe that he would ever be able to become a teacher. Zeke was so shy; he was convinced that he would never become a teacher. Zeke's dad would often say (to neighbors and friends), "Do you know what Zeke is thinking, he never talks."

Even though Zeke was 'quiet & shy,' he was very excited about 'exploring' and discovering treasures. Zeke knew that he was 'special' and that Nature would show him its treasures. When Zeke went to bed tonight, he knew that he would be dreaming about the next treasure that he would find in his hometown. Zeke also knew that as soon as he hopped onto his bed (tonight), he would hear his older brother (Zack) yell: "Zeke, did the monsters get you!?"

Every night was the same. Every night 'Little Zeke' would go upstairs to bed first (because he was the youngest child in his family). Every night Zeke would hear his brother yelling (from downstairs), "Zeke! Zeke! Answer me! Did the Monsters get you? Did the Monsters eat you?" If Zeke was awake or if he wanted to annoy his brother, he would respond: "No Zack, the monsters didn't eat me! The monsters are waiting for you to come upstairs. The monsters want to eat you because they know that you are afraid of them."

Zeke knew that he would be dreaming about 'treasures.' Whenever Zeke wasn't playing a game or a sport, his mind was 'racing & thinking;' his mind was often thinking about discovering treasures. Tonight and every night, 'Little Zeke' would dream about: "Finding treasures and aiding Nature or someone who needed help."

When Zeke awoke, the next morning, he remembered dreaming about: "Invasive species and how Mr. Henry helped his town adapt to an Invasive species. Zeke also remembered members of his family being called an 'invasive species.' Then Zeke remembered Uncle Eddie saying: "Zeke, you are very lucky to have Mr. Henry as your neighbor; he's the perfect neighbor."

After eating breakfast, Zeke asked his mom if he could go down to the creek with Billy. Zeke's mom said, "Zekie, you can play with Billy everyday; he's such a nice boy! Just be home at dinner time." Zeke responded, "Thanks mom! I know that I'm going to discover another treasure; Nature will lead me to another treasure! Mr. Hill said that I'm special and that Nature will show me all of her treasures." Zeke's mom responded, "Zekie, you are special; all children are special and all children have gifts to share. Have fun exploring, but don't bring home any snakes; you know that I don't like snakes." Zeke responded, "OK mom!"

Zeke's mind was thinking about what Uncle Eddie talked about yesterday. Zeke was thinking about Gypsy moth caterpillars being invasive species and killing the forest trees. Zeke was going to look in the woods for examples of 'dead trees.' Zeke wanted to look at a dead tree; he wanted to answer Uncle Eddie's question: "Is a dead tree really dead?"

Zeke walked over to Billy's house and asked him if he wanted to go exploring. Billy responded, "Sure! Let's go down to the creek; I'll bring my net and a bucket. Maybe we can catch a turtle or some frogs."

Zeke was happy and excited about exploring with his best friend Billy and he believed that Nature would lead him to its next treasure. When Zeke and Billy got to the creek, Zeke said: "Billy, let's look for some dead trees. Uncle Eddie asked me the silliest question. He asked me 'if a dead tree is really dead?' Isn't that a silly question?" Billy responded, "It sure is silly. Everybody knows that a dead tree is dead."

When Billy and Zeke crossed over the creek and started to walk into the woods Zeke said to Billy, "Billy, do you hear that weird noise? There's a weird noise. It sounds like a 'chewing sound.' Billy, do you hear it?" Billy responded, "I do hear it."

As Zeke and Billy looked up into the trees - to see if they could determine what was making the unusual sound that they heard, they felt something falling down on them.   Zeke and Billy both looked at their arms and said: "What is that black stuff that's on our arms? What is falling out of the trees? Those little black things are dropping out of the trees."

Zeke then said to Billy, "Let's get away from those trees; I don't like that black stuff falling on me. I see a dead tree near the creek bend. I really want to look at it so that I can tell Uncle Eddie what I saw - when I looked at a dead tree."

While walking towards the 'dead tree' that was in the forest, Zeke passed several trees that had 'carvings' in them. Zeke said to Billy, "Billy, look what the mean kids did to those trees; they carved letters into the tree. Why would people hurt the tree? Why would people carve letters into a tree's bark? Do you think that it (the carved letters) will kill the tree?" Billy responded, "Teenagers carve those letters into trees. When a boy likes a girl, he will carve a heart shape into a tree and then he will put his initials and the girl that he likes initials inside of the heart shaped carving. Zeke, see that one heart shaped carving; inside of the heart are the initials: 'R. D. & D. J.' --- I think that Richie carved those letters into the tree. Richie likes Donna."

Zeke responded, "That's stupid. Why would you want to hurt a tree? Shouldn't Richie just tell Donna that he likes her or loves her? Is that what 'bully teenagers' do? I know that I wouldn't do that to any tree." Billy responded, "I wouldn't carve initials into a tree either, but I do like to climb in trees and swing from trees. When you and I are a little bigger we can make a 'tree fort;' and you can keep your treasures in it." Zeke responded, "Billy, I can't wait until I'm big enough to make a tree fort with you. I would put my treasures in it; we could put lots of 'neat things' in it."

Before reaching the dead tree that Zeke wanted to study and look carefully at, he saw an unusual carving in a tree's bark. Zeke said to Billy, "Look at this carving Billy. There are letters but there isn't any heart shape. The letters: 'CTG' & 'BTG' are carved into this tree's bark. This carving must mean something special. The carving on this tree must be a code. Billy, take a picture of this tree carving. It has an arrow too - in the carving; it says: 'CTG > BTG.' Billy, make sure that you get the arrow shape in your cell phone picture. We can show Uncle Eddie the picture. I'm sure that he will know what those letters mean."

After Billy took a picture of the tree carving, Zeke decided to sit on a 'fallen tree log' and look at a dead tree that was nearby. Zeke wasn't sure if Uncle Eddie was tricking him or serious when he asked him: 'if a dead tree is really dead.'

Zeke was amazed at what he saw when he looked at a 'dead tree' - that was still standing. Zeke saw: 'Woodpeckers - pecking at the dead tree; he saw other birds pecking at it too; he saw animals nesting in it; he saw weird & colorful mushrooms growing out of it; he saw an owl peeking out of a hole in the tree and he saw some baby mammals peeking out of another hole in the tree (he thought that they were baby raccoons).' Then Zeke thought: "Maybe Uncle Eddie wasn't asking a 'trick' question; maybe he was serious." While sitting on a 'dead tree' log, Zeke saw many other interesting things; he saw lots of ants; the ants were burrowing into the decaying log; he also saw beetles and mushrooms on the log. Zeke decided to poke at the log. When Zeke poked at the decaying log, a big piece of wood came off. Zeke saw dozens of termites inside of the decaying log.

Zeke was excited and he wanted to tell Uncle Eddie what he saw when he looked at a dead tree. Zeke now knew the answer to Uncle Eddie's question. Zeke now knew that a dead tree isn't really dead but that it is another form of life; a dead tree is food, housing and energy for other life forms. Zeke wanted to tell Uncle Eddie, but Zeke also wanted to ask Uncle Eddie what the unusual letters (CTG > BTG) meant. Zeke knew that they meant something special, and he believed that Uncle Eddie would know what they meant. Zeke now knew that Uncle Eddie was special (like Mr. Hill) and that he knew a lot about Nature. Zeke also believed that Uncle Eddie would know what that 'black stuff' was --- that fell out of the trees onto Zeke and Billy.

Zeke believed that an 'invasive species' created that 'black stuff' that was falling out of the trees; so Zeke said to Billy: "Billy, let's go see Uncle Eddie and show him your picture of the tree carvings; I'm sure he will know what it means. Uncle Eddie will also know what that black stuff was; that black stuff was really yucky." Billy responded, "I'm sure that you are right and we can have some of his candy. He always has candy and he loves to share it with us. He's so nice! Let's go!"

****

13. The Perfect Neighbor

When Zeke and Billy got back to Billy's house they put Billy's net & bucket in Billy's garage then they washed the 'black stuff' off of their arms. As soon as Zeke and

Billy walked out of Billy's front door they saw Uncle Eddie. Uncle Eddie was working in his yard. Uncle Eddie loved gardening and taking care of his lawn. He truly had the most beautiful lawn in the town.

Zeke yelled, "Uncle Eddie, I know the answer to your question. I looked at a dead tree. I know the answer, but I have some questions for you." Uncle Eddie responded, "Come on over; I'll gladly answer your questions." Billy then yelled, "Uncle Eddie, do you have any candy that Zeke and I can have?" Eddie responded, "Billy, you know that I always have candy and I love to share it with you two and all of the neighborhood children. All children are 'special' and all of the kids in this neighborhood are wonderful kids!"

Zeke had so many questions to ask Uncle Eddie. The first question that he asked was: "Uncle Eddie why do you love gardening? You're always outside working in your garden. Eddie looked at Zeke and said: "First, I want to tell you my gardening poem. I want you to hear it and one day I'll explain it. Just as I asked you to think about whether a 'dead tree is really dead;' Listen carefully to my poem. One day I'll write it down for you."

"Gardeners Know"

Gardeners know --- how to scatter & sow.

Gardeners know --- how to make things grow.

Gardeners know - that they must 'care lovingly' for their seedlings.

Gardeners know that they must be 'patient' as Nature has its own timing.

Loving gardeners - 'grow more beautiful inside' ---

as they 'scatter & sow' - a new crop of seeds.

Gardeners know - how to live --- 'joyfully!'

Zeke looked at Uncle Eddie and said, "Uncle Eddie, you talk just like Mr. Hill. I have no idea what you mean when you say: 'gardeners know' & Nature having its own timing. Let me tell you what Billy and I discovered in the woods today."

Zeke told Uncle Eddie that he and Billy heard an unusual noise, as soon as they got to the woods. Zeke said, "When Billy and I looked up into the trees, to see what the noise was, this 'black stuff' started falling down from the trees. This 'black stuff' was really 'yucky.' Billy and I got away from those trees and I sat on a log and looked at a dead tree that was still standing in the woods. I know the answer to your question. The answer is that a 'dead tree' isn't really dead. A dead tree is another form of life; am I right? Is that the answer to your question?"

Eddie looked at Zeke and said: "Zeke, you are right. Dead trees are life forms for other living things. Nature never wastes. <u>Nature always recycles and reuses its energy</u>. Everything is energy, but many people waste their energy."

Zeke responded, "I don't know what you mean about Nature recycling or that everything is energy, but I saw lots of things living in the dead tree and lots of things using the dead tree. Uncle Eddie, what was that 'black stuff' that was falling out of the trees; that yucky stuff got all over my arms --- it was really yucky."

Eddie looked at Zeke and Billy then said: "The noise that you heard, in the woods, was Gypsy Moth caterpillars; you heard them chewing the leaves. When there are thousands of them in the trees, you can hear them chewing. And the 'black stuff' that was dropping from the trees, onto you two, was 'caterpillar poop.' Caterpillar poop is 'yucky.' Those caterpillars will 'totally defoliate' the trees; they will eat every leaf off of the trees. They will kill the trees. Trees can't survive and live without leaves. The tree's leaves make food for the trees."

Zeke looked at Eddie then said: "That's disgusting! Billy and I got 'pooped' on. I thought that tree leaves were just meant to shade the trees; how can leaves make food? I don't understand how leaves can make food, but I have another question for you. Billy and I saw trees that had letters carved into them. Uncle Eddie, does it kill the tree when someone carves letters into it? We saw heart shaped carvings with letters inside the heart shape and one carving was unusual; it just had the letter: CTG > BTG. I think that 'CTG > BTG' is a special code; it must mean something. What could it mean?"

Eddie looked at Zeke, then said: "Nature is teaching you Zeke. You are learning quickly. You are a great student and very observant. One day I will explain how leaves make food for the trees; it's called 'Photosynthesis.' The leaves use the sun's light and make sugar. I think that you are right about the carvings on the one tree; I think that Nature wanted you to: 'see & be.' The first letter (C), really means: 'see.' The first letter after the > (B) means: 'be.' What you see --- you be. <u>What you see, you be.</u> If you see the beauty that is all around you, you become more beautiful. If you see 'ugly' then you become ugly. So, the carved letters: 'CTG > BTG' mean: 'See the good and be the good.' Nature wants you to see all of its beauty then share that beauty with others. Just as leaves make 'sweet food' with the help of sunlight. Little Zeke, you can make people's lives 'sweeter & more beautiful' by teaching them to see like you. Those who can 'see the beauty' that is all around, make everyone they meet feel good; they make everyone's day better."

Zeke looked at Eddie and said: "I don't understand about leaves making sugar or much of what you said, but I do see beauty in tiny little things. All of Nature is beautiful to me and I always try to help Nature and people who need help. So are you saying that I am 'sweet food' for my friends and neighbors. Do I make my friends and neighbors life's - sweeter and better?"

Eddie responded, "Zeke, you sure do make everyone's life - sweeter & better; just by being you. You truly have a '<u>unique nature</u>.' Zeke, just continue to be 'yourself' and let Nature teach you." Then Eddie said: "Zeke, the carvings into the bark of trees don't kill the trees, but it's not good for the trees. Most trees will heal from the 'carving wound;' it's like you getting 'cut or scratched' - your skin creates a scab and heals the cut. Nature will heal and adapt to every challenge. Some things will die but Nature will go on --- it will survive.

Remember, Charles Darwin said: 'It's not the strongest that will survive, it's the ones who are the most adaptable to change.' Nature will adapt to the invasive species, like the Gypsy Moths. Humans think that they are smarter than Nature. Humans think that they can control everything and solve every problem. Some 'rich & powerful' humans want to control all of Nature. Nature won't be controlled but it can teach us how to: 'survive & thrive.' Just as the forests have to adapt to invasive species, so too do people and towns. Our town is 'thriving' because it has 'kind and caring' people. Mr. Henry is a great example of: Darwin's theory. Mr. Henry showed his neighborhood how to adapt.

Long ago, this town wanted only Germans to live in it. Mr. Henry saw the 'goodness' in all of his neighbors. Mr. Henry was kind and helpful to all of his neighbors. He showed all of his neighbors how to 'treat each other.' Your parents and grandparents were Italians and considered an 'invasive species.' The German founders in this town didn't want any Italians, or Irish or Jewish or other ethnicities living in their town. Mr. Henry didn't care what a persons 'ethnicity' was. Mr. Henry just saw the 'beauty & goodness' of his neighbors.

Mr. Henry aided everyone. He was always helping his neighbors. Mr. Henry would plow the snow off of the sidewalks of his neighbors. He would bring truck loads of potatoes back from Maine and share them with his neighbors. One time when he plowed the snow from his neighbors sidewalks, his plow damaged several sidewalks. Mr. Henry brought his cement truck and replaced the damaged sidewalks. Mr. Henry was always helping people and he was a very funny man. He added a lot of 'sweetness' to his neighborhood; he was: 'the perfect neighbor.' Your dad and Mr. Henry became very good friends.

Mr. Henry could 'see' - 'the beauty in diversity'. Nature and the woods are filled with diversity; there are many species living in harmony. Mr. Henry (of German ancestry) became good friends with your dad (of Italian ancestry).

Zeke, you and Billy are similar to Mr. Henry & your dad. Billy is of German ancestry and you are half Italian and half Scottish. Zeke, remember this: 'Friendship is color blind.' Friends don't care about religion, or ancestry. Friends just like being together and having fun together.

Mr. Henry is 'special.' He knows how to 'see and be' --- he 'sees' the beauty & goodness that is all around him and he is a beautiful person. You are very lucky to have Mr. Henry as your next door neighbor.

Zeke looked at Uncle Eddie and said: "Mr. Henry is my favorite neighbor; he really is nice. He must be an 'Omegan,' but I don't think that he likes bats. Sometimes bats get into his attic and his wife (Mrs. Lillian) and his daughters (Joyce & Carol) will scream. Joyce will tell me whenever they have bats in their attic. She said that bats will make a nest in girls' long hair. Uncle Eddie, do bats make nests in people's hair?"

Eddie looked at Zeke, then said: "No Zeke, bats don't make nests in people's hair; that's a myth. Bats are very good; they eat thousands of pestie bugs; they can eat 3000 mosquitoes in one night. Bats also help pollinate flowers; many fruits are pollinated by bats. One day I'll tell you about bats. Enjoy exploring and learning about Nature; and enjoy having a wonderful friend, like Billy."

****

*Friendship truly is color blind. Friends don't care about the race, ethnicity or the religion of their friend(s); they simply enjoy sharing time together.

14. The Phone in the Woods

After listening to Uncle Eddie talking about invasive species and Nature adapting to everything, Zeke knew that Nature was going to teach him and show him more treasures. Zeke knew that he would be dreaming tonight; he knew that tonight he would dream about the next treasure that he would find in his hometown. But Zeke knew that he would also be thinking about 'caterpillar poop.'

As soon as Zeke hopped onto his bed he heard a voice from below; he heard the usual bedtime sound. Zeke's older brother Zack was yelling (from downstairs), "Zeke, Zeke! Did the monsters get you? Answer me! Did the monsters eat you?" Zeke didn't answer because he was sleeping and dreaming about treasures.

When Zeke awoke the next morning, he was convinced that he would find another treasure. Zeke quickly ate his morning cereal, then said: "Mom, can I go exploring with Billy? I know that I will find a new treasure today. Nature always leads me to treasures." Zeke's mom responded, "Sure, you can go exploring with Billy. But remember, don't bring home any snakes; just be home for dinner."
Zeke responded, "Thanks mom!" Then Zeke started to think about where to look for his next treasure. While thinking about finding his next treasure, Zeke heard a knock on his front door; it was Billy. As soon as Zeke opened the door, Billy said: "Zeke, let's go exploring; maybe you'll find another treasure. You have a 'knack' for finding treasures." Zeke said: "Thanks Billy. We always have fun together; you're my best friend."

When Zeke and Billy got to the creek, Zeke's mind told him to go back to the mud puddle (that had special mud). Zeke told Billy that he wanted to go back to the 'special mud puddle'. Billy looked at Zeke and said, "I'm not walking through the briar patch; I'm not getting scratched and cut. You had cuts and scratches all over your body."

Zeke looked at Billy and said: "We'll find another way to the 'special mud puddle.' As Zeke and Billy were walking past the briar patch, Zeke saw a Box turtle. Zeke said,

"Billy, let's stop and look at that Box turtle; maybe that's Earl. Maybe that's the Box turtle that we rescued and returned to the woods."

As soon as Zeke and Billy got to the Box turtle, it went into its shell. Zeke picked it up. Zeke noticed that it wasn't Earl, but he saw something unusual on the turtle's shell. Zeke said to Billy, "Billy, this isn't Earl (our turtle), but look at its shell. This turtle has an unusual etching on its shell; it has the same shape as the one on my special key. I'm going to touch that shape with my special key. I'm sure that this turtle will lead us to another treasure."

When Zeke touched the turtle's shell with his skeleton key, that part of the turtle's shell opened up. Zeke took out his green sea glass and looked at the open part of the turtle's shell. While looking through the green sea glass, Zeke saw a piece of paper, then he said: "Billy, do you have your 'Swiss Army' tool?" Billy responded, "Yeah!" Billy then handed it to Zeke.

Zeke used the Swiss Army tool to pull out the 'piece of paper,' that was under the turtle's shell. As soon as Zeke got the 'folded up piece of paper' from the turtle's shell, he gently put the turtle onto the ground.

As soon as the turtle was placed on the ground, the part of the shell that had opened - closed up. Then the turtle stuck its neck out and looked at Zeke. Zeke was amazed that the turtle turned and looked at him. Then Zeke's mind thought: "Zeke, you have a special connection to Nature. Nature will teach you and show you its treasures."

Billy then said, "Zeke, are you watching this turtle? It's looking at you then it's turning its head. It's using its head to point in the direction to your left. I think it's telling us to go to your left. Look! Now it's walking in that direction."

Zeke looked at the Box turtle and smiled. The turtle looked at Zeke and smiled back at Zeke, then began walking into the woods. Zeke looked at Billy and said, "Billy, you're right; the turtle was telling us to go to my left. I think that our next treasure is in that direction. But before we go, I want to look at this piece of paper that was under the turtle's shell."

Billy looked at Zeke and said, "That's a good idea." Then he said: "Zeke, I think that turtle smiled at you. After you smiled at the turtle, it looked like it smiled at you. Zeke, you really do have a 'special connection' with Nature." Zeke looked at Billy then said, "Billy, it did smile at me. I know that we are going to find another treasure today."

Zeke then opened the folded up piece of paper (that was under the turtle's shell). The printing on the paper was very tiny, so Zeke decided to look at it through his green sea glass. The green sea glass was a magnifier. When Zeke looked through the sea glass, he could read the note. The note said: "Look in the mud puddle; look through your sea glass."

Zeke turned to Billy and said: "The note is telling us to go to the mud puddle and that I should use my sea glass to look into the mud puddle. Let's follow the turtle."

Zeke and Billy followed the turtle and it led them to a path that went directly to the 'special mud puddle.' The turtle showed them how to get to the special mud puddle without getting cut & scratched by briars.

When they got to the mud puddle, the turtle turned and looked at Zeke. It pointed three times to the mud puddle then smiled at Zeke. Zeke smiled and nodded to the turtle (as if to say - Thanks for showing us the way).

As the turtle walked into the woods, Billy said: "Zeke, I can't believe it; that turtle smiled at you again. Before it walked into the woods it smiled at you. I know it did." Zeke then looked at Billy and said, "Billy, I'm going to call that turtle Megan. It had an 'Omega' symbol on its shell. My skeleton key has an 'Omega' symbol on it. Billy, do you like the name Meg or Megan?" Billy responded, "That's a good name. She can be our Irish Box turtle. We can call her O'Megan. A lot of Irish people have names that start with the letter O."

Zeke looked at Billy then said, "I like the name: O'Megan. I am an Omega and you are too, Billy. All Nature lovers are Omegans." Then Zeke gave Megan (the Box turtle) one last look and nod.

Now it was time to find the treasure that was in the mud puddle. So Zeke took out his green sea glass and began looking through it. Zeke had a plan; he was going to scan the whole mud puddle while looking through the sea glass. Zeke thought that he should first look in the center of the mud puddle.

While looking at the center of the mud puddle Zeke saw an object. Zeke looked again and could see that it was a phone. Zeke then said, "Billy, there's a phone in the mud puddle. Give me your net. I can reach it with your net."

Billy handed Zeke his net and Zeke retrieved the phone from the mud puddle. Billy looked at Zeke then said, "Someone must have lost their phone, I'm sure that it doesn't work. Phones don't work when they are under water."

Zeke looked at Billy then said, "You're probably right. But I'm going to wipe off all of the mud then push the power button." As soon as Zeke pushed the power button, the phone screen lit up. Then Zeke saw a message on the phone screen. The phone screen had: '? U C U B' on it.

Zeke's mind instantly thought: "I've seen or heard those letters before." But Zeke couldn't recall where he had heard or seen those letters. Then the screen went blank. The phone screen turned off.

Zeke then looked at Billy and said, "Uncle Eddie would know what those letters mean. Let's show Uncle Eddie what we found." Billy looked at Zeke and said, "Yeah, let's go see Uncle Eddie. I want some of his candy. He always has candy and he loves to share it with us."

It was a beautiful day and Uncle Eddie was outside; he was working in his garden. Zeke walked up to Uncle Eddie and said, "Uncle Eddie, I found another treasure in the woods. I found a cellphone and strange letters showed up on the phone when I pushed the power button."

Eddie looked at Zeke and said, "What letters showed up on the phone. Tell me exactly what you saw on the phone." Zeke responded, "There was a question mark, then the letters: U, C, U and B. I know that I saw those letters before but I can't remember where."

Eddie looked at Zeke and said: "I didn't say those letters to you, but we talked about what they mean. We talked about Mr. Henry being able to 'see.' Mr. Henry could see the 'good' in his neighbors. We talked about 'seeing' and 'being.' This is a follow-up to the tree carving message. Remember Zeke, you showed me the tree carving letters: 'CTG > BTG;' which means: 'See the Good and Be the Good.' Your phone text message means: 'What you see, you be.' The question mark means: (what), the letter U means: (you) the letter C means: (see) and the letter B means: (be). If you see the good in others, then you will extend goodness and kindness to others. If you see 'ugly' or the worst in others then you will become ugly or a 'negative' person."

After listening to Eddie, Zeke remembered where he had seen those letters. Zeke then said: "Uncle Eddie, those letters were on the Oyster shells that I found on the beach last summer. I gave those Oyster shells to my favorite Aunt. My aunt Id loves those Oyster shells and has them on her coffee table. Mr. Hill told me the same thing. He said those letters mean what you said. My dad told me: 'to always look for the good in other people; he said that if I see the best in others then I will become better; he said that there's good in everyone.' My dad also said: 'It takes two to argue but that it only takes one to end an argument. My dad says that a lot because my brother Zack and I are always fighting. He punches me every day and sometimes it really hurts."

Eddie looked at Zeke and said, "I know that Zack can be rough and he likes to prove that he is a 'tough guy,' but he's not a bully; he's not mean like Bruiser." Then Eddie looked at Zeke and said, "Zeke, let me look at the cellphone that you found."

Zeke handed the phone to Eddie and Eddie pushed the power button. As soon as Eddie pushed the power button, the phone screen lit up; then Zeke saw the screen covered with ones and zeros. The whole screen looked like a bunch of ones and zeros connected together. It looked like: 100110010010011100110.

Zeke looked at Eddie and said, "Uncle Eddie, that must be a secret code; it must mean something. What do all of those ones and zeros mean?" Eddie looked at Zeke and said, "Zeke, it is a code. Those are binary numbers. Computers show things in binary numbers. Computers have their own language or code. The arrangement of the ones and Zeros do mean something, but I don't know what. My nephew has a friend who is a computer expert. Can I give this phone to my nephew?"

Zeke responded, "Sure Uncle Eddie, you can give my phone to your nephew. Now your nephew has two things to find out. Let me know if he finds out what those ones and zeros mean. Thanks for telling me what those letters mean. A Box turtle told me where the cellphone was, and the Box turtle had an Omega symbol on its shell. Billy and I gave the turtle a name; we decided to call her Megan or (O' Megan) - since she had an Omega symbol on her shell; she's our Irish Box turtle."

Eddie looked at Zeke and said, "That's a cute name for a turtle. Then Eddie said, "Many Irish people changed the spelling of their last names; many stopped using the letter 'O.' The Irish people were considered an 'Invasive species;' they were afraid that people wouldn't give them jobs - so many lied when they were asked if they were Irish. Many Italians changed the spelling of their last names too - for the same reason.

One day you can tell me how Megan led you to this phone." Before Zeke could answer, Billy said: "Uncle Eddie, the turtle smiled at Zeke too. Can we have some candy; you always have candy and you love to share it with us. I want to play catch with Zeke before dinner."

Eddie looked at Billy and said: "Help yourself to some candy from the bowl that's on the porch; I'm going to work in my garden. Have fun playing catch. It's always nice to see you two; you're such good friends and nice boys, too!"

****

15. The Mystery Egg

When Zeke hopped into bed tonight he knew that he would be thinking and dreaming about Megan the turtle and the next treasure that he would find. When Zeke awoke the next morning, he remembered part of last night's dream. Zeke remembered seeing Maya (Ben's special pigeon). In Zeke's dream Maya landed on Zeke's shoulder, while he was exploring in the woods.

Zeke quickly ate his breakfast (a bowl of Frosted Flakes), then said: "Mom, can I go exploring with Billy? I know that I'm going to find another treasure today." Zack was eating breakfast with Zeke and said, "Mom, Zeke is a storyteller. He makes up stuff; all he ever finds is junk. He finds broken stuff and says that it's a treasure."

Zeke looked at Zack and said, "I do too find treasures. Nature leads me to its treasures because I am special and help Nature." Zack responded, "You're just a little kid who makes up stories."

Before Zeke could answer Zack, Zeke's mom said, "Zekie, have fun exploring with Billy, but don't bring home any snakes." Zeke responded, "Thanks Mom!" Zeke's mom was glad for the 'peace & quiet;' there never was any 'peace or quiet' in the house when Zack and Zeke were together.

Zeke was excited about finding the next treasure; he went and got Billy then said, "Billy, I know that I'm going to find another treasure. I dreamed last night that I found another treasure. Let's go exploring." Billy said, "OK, let's go."

Zeke told Billy to bring his rope ladder today. Zeke thought that he might find a treasure in a tree. When they got to the woods, Zeke said to Billy, "Let's go back to the path that led us to the mud puddle and to the opening in the woods. I remember seeing a few dead trees in my dream." Billy said, "Ok, but I'm not walking through any briars; I don't want to get cut or scratched."

When Zeke and Billy got to the special mud puddle, Zeke said: "Billy, I want to look at the mud puddle through my sea glass - to see if there are any more treasures; you can make a few mud pies while I'm looking through my sea glass." Billy said, "Ok, making mud pies is a lot of fun."

Zeke didn't see any treasures in the mud puddle, but Billy made a dozen mud pies and put them into his bucket. Zeke and Billy left the mud puddle and continued walking into the woods. The path led them to a clearing in the woods. Inside of the clearing were several dead trees. Zeke's mind thought: 'An invasive species must have killed those trees.'

When Zeke walked into the clearing, he heard a sound; he knew that it was the sound of a bird - when it's flying. Suddenly, Zeke felt something land on his shoulder. He looked and saw a white pigeon. Billy yelled: "Zeke, there's a white pigeon on your shoulder."

As soon as Zeke looked at the pigeon he knew who it was. Zeke extended his arm and the pigeon leaped onto Zeke's hand. Zeke looked at the pigeon and said, "Hi Maya. You flew a long way to see me. You must have a message for me." Then Maya nodded. Zeke took out his skeleton key that had an Omega symbol on it. Zeke touched Maya's leg band with the Omega symbol on his key; Maya's leg band opened and Zeke took out a piece of paper. As soon as Zeke took out the note (from Maya's leg band), Maya flew away.

Billy couldn't believe what he just saw. Billy looked at Zeke and said: "That beautiful white pigeon came out of nowhere and it landed on your shoulder. Then you touched its leg band and it opened and gave you a note. Zeke you are special and it's so much fun exploring with you. Look and see what the note says."

Zeke unfolded the note. There was a lot of printing but it was very tiny. Zeke knew that he would need his magnifier - his green sea glass. So Zeke looked at the note through his green sea glass. The note said: "3,4,5, right triangle…the log cabin was torn down...Sandy was sad but is safe."

Zeke looked at Billy and said, "Billy, do you know what a right triangle is?" Billy looked at Zeke and said, "Kinda. I'll draw you one in the sand." Then Billy drew a right triangle in the sand.

Zeke looked at the triangle then looked at the dead trees. Zeke saw that some of the dead trees were like a right triangle; they were like the corners of right triangles. Then Zeke thought, "find three dead trees that make a right triangle shape."

Zeke stood next to one tree then walked three (3)paces; then Zeke turned and walked four (4) paces; that brought Zeke to another dead tree; then Zeke turned and walked five (5) paces; that brought him to another dead tree.

Zeke's mind was racing and thinking: 'there must be a treasure somewhere in this triangle.' While Zeke stood next to the tree he heard a 'cooing' sound. Zeke instantly knew that it was the sound of a pigeon. Zeke looked up and saw Maya.

Maya was sitting on top of a birdhouse. The birdhouse was attached to the dead tree. Zeke couldn't reach the birdhouse from the ground, so he yelled to Billy, "Billy, bring your rope ladder. I know that there is a treasure in that birdhouse. Maya is sitting on top of that birdhouse."

Maya flew away and Zeke tossed the rope ladder over a branch that was near the birdhouse. When Zeke climbed up the rope ladder he saw a lock on the birdhouse. The lock had an Omega symbol on it; Zeke knew that his special key would open it. Zeke took three (3) deep breaths; he was so excited.

Zeke's key fit perfectly into the lock. Zeke turned his key and then took off the lock. Zeke thought that he would see a bird sitting on a nest; he was wrong. Zeke just stared, as he looked into the opened birdhouse. Billy yelled to Zeke, he said, "Zeke! What did you find? Tell me!"

Zeke was stunned and amazed, he stared for a few more seconds then he touched the object that was inside of the birdhouse. Zeke saw a beautiful bird's egg, so he touched it gently; he didn't want to break it. When Zeke touched the egg, he felt that it was hard; it was hard as a rock.

Zeke's mind was racing again, it was thinking: 'maybe it's a petrified egg; maybe it's a dinosaur egg from millions of years ago.' Zeke gently picked up the egg and looked at it. He looked down at Billy and said, "Billy, I found an egg, but it's hard as a rock. I'll show you when I get down." Zeke put the lock back on the birdhouse and came down the rope ladder.

When Zeke got down he said, "Billy, take a picture of that birdhouse. I want to show Uncle Eddie what we found." Zeke then handed the egg to Billy.

Billy looked at the egg and said, "It is hard as a rock. It's beautiful! It has amazing colors, too." Then Billy gave Zeke the egg and Zeke looked again at the egg and said, "Billy, there's someone's face on the egg. I see someone's face imprinted in the egg. I know that Maya led me to this treasure. I know that this is special and that the face means something. Maybe Uncle Eddie will know why this egg is hard and why there's a face on it."

Billy looked at Zeke and said, "Zeke, you are amazing! You always find 'neat' things. You do have a 'special connection' to Nature. I love exploring with you; you're my best friend. Let's go get some of Uncle Eddie's candy. He always has candy and he loves to share it - with us."

While walking to Uncle Eddie's, Zeke's mind was 'racing;' it was thinking about what was on Maya's note. Zeke's mind was thinking about the log cabin and Sandy. Zeke suddenly felt very sad; thinking about Sandy and the log cabin made Zeke worry.

When Zeke and Billy got back to Billy's house, Billy's mom said: "Billy, I have to go to the store, you'll have to come with me. You can play with Zeke tomorrow."

When Billy went to the store, with his mom, Zeke walked across the street to Uncle Eddie's house. Uncle Eddie wasn't working in his garden or in his yard so Zeke walked home. When Zeke got home, he saw Mr. Henry. Mr. Henry was getting out of his car and he had a bunch of flowers in his hand.

Zeke looked at Mr. Henry and said, "Mr. Henry, why do you always bring flowers home? Where do you get the flowers from? Do you have a secret garden where you work?

Mr.Henry laughed as he looked at Zeke, then said: "Zeke, I don't have a secret flower garden. I bring the flowers home from funerals. I'm in the burial business and people leave flowers on the graves and around the graves of their loved ones who have died. After each burial, my workers have to cover (fill in) the graves with soil. The flowers would be destroyed and the cemetery caretakers throw out all of the flowers that are left in the cemetery. Lillian, my wife, loves flowers. I bring them home to her.

Zeke looked at Mr. Henry and said, "Oh. You and Mrs. Lillian are my favorite neighbors. Uncle Eddie told me that you are: 'the perfect neighbor.' He said that you help everybody. He said that you are kind and nice to everybody. He said that I am very lucky to have you as my neighbor. Mr. Henry, do you want to see what I found in the woods? Nature leads me to treasures."

Henry smiled and laughed as Zeke was talking about Uncle Eddie's stories. Then Henry said, "Zeke, let me see what you found." Zeke handed the egg shaped object to Mr. Henry and the note. Then Zeke said, "Mr. Ben's special pigeon gave me the note and showed me where this hard egg was. Mr. Ben is kind like you Mr.Henry. Mr. Ben is called: the 'pearl man' and Benevolent Ben."

Henry looked at Zeke and said, "I know Ben the jeweler; he made a pearl necklace for my wife. Lil loves her pearls. I'm going to see Ben in a few days. I need him to fix Lil's pearl necklace. Zeke, would you like to come with me when I go to Ben's jewelry store?"

Zeke responded, "I would love to go see Mr. Ben. I want to give him some of my special mud; he can use it to polish his special pearls. Mr. Ben makes healing necklaces for sick children. I have questions to ask him, too. I need to know if Sandy is okay and what happened to the log cabin. Mr. Henry, you should ask Mr. Ben to use his 'special pearl string' when he fixes Mrs. Lillian's necklace. Mr. Ben has a special pearl string; it's shiny and will last forever. I know where he gets it but I can't tell you. Mr. Ben might tell you Mr. Henry."

Henry smiled whenever Little Zeke told him his stories, then Henry said: "Zeke, this is an amazing find. Your egg is like a 'petrified rock;' it's like a gem. It also has a person's profile etched into the stone. Zeke, there are lots of buried treasures; I sometimes find old things when I am digging a grave. Would you like me to give you some of the things that I find when I dig graves?"

Zeke looked at Mr. Henry and said, "I'd love to have any treasures that you find under the ground. I can't wait to go and see Mr. Ben, thanks for offering to take me; you really are my favorite neighbor. The man who lives on the other side of our house is mean and cranky. He keeps our balls, if they go into his yard. He also lets his big dog out, if we climb over the fence and try to get our balls out of his yard. His dog is named 'Happy,' but he's mean and vicious. All of the kids on the block are afraid of Happy. Mr. Hill's dog is nice, but Zack is afraid of him. Mr. Henry, do you know Mr. Hill?"

Henry looked at Zeke and laughed (when hearing about the mean dog named Happy), then he said: "I don't know Mr. Hill, but your brother Zack is crazy. Today, I saw him shooting arrows straight up into the air. I stopped and told him how dangerous that was. Zack said that he was quick enough to get out of the way, before the arrow came down. Zeke, never shoot arrows straight up into the air, it's very dangerous; only shoot arrows at the bull's eye targets on your hay bales." Zeke responded, "Ok Mr. Henry. I'm not goofy like Zack. Let me know when you're going to take me to see Mr. Ben; I can't wait. Thanks again! Does Mrs. Lillian know that the flowers that you give her are dead people's flowers?" Henry smiled and laughed, then said: "Yes, she knows."

****

16. The Garden of Good

Zeke knew that when he went to bed tonight that he would be dreaming about finding more treasures. Zeke was also excited about treasures that Mr, Henry might find when he digs graves. Before falling asleep tonight Zeke was thinking about the many things that he wanted to ask Mr. Ben. Zeke was excited about seeing Mr. Ben and Maya (Ben's special pigeon), but Zeke was also worried and sad when he looked at the note and it said that Sandy was sad. Zeke knew that Mr. Ben or Mr. Hill would be able to tell him what happened to Sandy. But Zeke's thoughts about Sandy were interrupted by yelling from downstairs.

Zack was yelling (from downstairs) to Zeke. Every night was the same; Zack would yell: "Zeke! Answer me! Did the monsters eat you?" Tonight Zeke decided to say, "No Zack, I just saw five monsters go under your bed; they're waiting to eat you because they know that you're a scaredy cat!"

The next morning, Zeke ate his bowl of cereal (he ate Wheaties - the breakfast of champions); he was sure that he would find more treasures and was excited about going to see Mr. Ben. As soon as Zeke finished his breakfast Zeke's mom said, "Zeke, Billy's here; he wants to play with you. It's a beautiful day; play outside."

Zeke grabbed his baseball glove, and the egg shaped object that he discovered in the tree. Zeke wanted to show the egg and the note to Uncle Eddie. Zeke was sure that Uncle Eddie could explain why the egg was hard as a rock and why there was a person's face etched into it.

Zeke and Billy played an 'imaginary' game of baseball; they often played this game. Zeke was the pitcher and Billy would be the catcher. Zeke would 'wind up' and throw the ball to Billy. Billy would yell, "Ball or Strike;" depending on whether Zeke's pitches were balls or strikes. After playing catch for a long time, Billy said: "Let's go see if Uncle Eddie's in his yard, I want some candy; he always has candy." Zeke responded, "Yeah, let's go. I want to show him the egg that I found in the bird house."

Eddie was working in his yard. He was spreading dark stuff all over his beautiful lawn. His lawn didn't look beautiful with that ugly stuff on top of it. Zeke yelled to Eddie, "Uncle Eddie, I want to show you the treasure that I found in the woods. I found an egg in a birdhouse but it's hard as a rock."

Eddie responded by saying: "Come on over; let me see your newest treasure." As soon as Billy and Zeke walked into Eddie's yard, Billy said: "Uncle Eddie, do you have any candy?" Eddie smiled and laughed, then said: "Billy, you know that I always have candy and I share it with the neighborhood kids; help yourself."

Zeke took the egg out of his pocket and handed it to Eddie. Eddie looked at the egg then said, "Zeke, this is beautiful. It is hard as a rock. I've never seen anything like this before. You said that you found this in a birdhouse. The colors on this egg are amazing and it has the profile of a person's face in it. A person's face is etched into it; this truly is a unique find."

Then Eddie proceeded to tell Zeke and Billy about people who love birds and Nature. He told them how some people will travel all over the world; just to be able to see a bird species that is rare or one that they've never seen.

Zeke learned that there are millions of bird lovers in the United States and that many species of birds are endangered; this made Zeke feel bad. Then Eddie told Zeke that many Nature lovers are building birdhouses and placing them in the woods, for birds to make nests in; that made Zeke happy. Eddie said that Wood Duck houses and Bluebird houses are often seen in the woods around here. Osprey platforms are made and put in the marsh areas (for Ospreys to nest in). The pesticide DDT killed many Ospreys and Eagles. Fortunately, people stopped using DDT; so now there are more Eagles and Ospreys. Ospreys and Eagles are beautiful birds.

Zeke looked at Eddie and said, "Uncle Eddie, that's great that so many people like birds and try to help them by making birdhouses. I want you to look at the note that Mr. Ben's pigeon gave me. The pigeon's name is Maya and she's special. She flew a long way and she showed me where the egg was. Do you know Mr. Ben? Before I show you my note, can you tell me why you put all of that black yucky stuff all over your lawn. You have the prettiest lawn in the whole town but now it doesn't look pretty; it looks yucky."

Eddie smiled as he thought about Zeke's comments, then said: "The black yucky stuff that I spread on my lawn is food; my lawn needs food to grow and to be healthy. My lawn gets its beautiful green color because I feed it; I give it healthy food. People need to eat healthy food to stay strong, so do plants. Some people use bags of fertilizer on their lawns and they over fertilize their lawns; this makes their lawns weak and not healthy. Then the extra fertilizer washes away into the streams and it kills fish. Too much fertilizer is bad for lawns. Eating too much food is bad for people too."

Zeke looked at Eddie and said, "Uncle Eddie, I don't see any bags of fertilizer. Where do you get your fertilizer from?" Eddie looked at Zeke and pointed to his compost pile & and his worm farm.

Then Eddie said, "Zeke, do you remember when I gave you and Billy a quarter for each big bag of leaves that you brought me last Fall?" Zeke said, "Yeah, that was nice. Billy and I bought a lot of candy. You paid us a whole dollar for those leaves."

Eddie then said, "My earthworms chewed up those leaves and made them into food for my lawn and flowers. I like to use natural food for my plants and lawn; people refer to that as 'Organic gardening.' Some people like to use pesticides too. Some people want to kill every bug they see. I don't like to use pesticides, because pesticides are harmful to bees. I love bees; they pollinate my flowers. We wouldn't have the food that I like to eat if we didn't have bees.

Nicotine is a poisonous pesticide that is used to kill bugs. Nicotine comes from the tobacco leaf. Tobacco is the only plant that has nicotine in it. Many people smoke or chew tobacco; it's very unhealthy for people.

Smoking cigarettes will kill you. A lot of my friends smoked cigarettes and they died from cancer or had heart attacks. I hope that you and Billy never smoke tobacco or vape. Today, a lot of kids are vaping. They're inhaling nicotine through heated pods. There's a lot of nicotine in each pod; don't ever vape or smoke cigarettes."

Zeke looked at Eddie and said, "I see those pods lying in the street. I guess kids throw them away; they just throw them in the street. It's not nice to litter. I don't plan on smoking. My mom smokes and it stinks but my dad doesn't smoke. My brother doesn't like bees, he knocked down a Hornets' nest in Ernie's barn and got stung. I didn't get stung because the Hornets knew that I'm nice to Nature."

Eddie laughed as Zeke explained why he didn't get stung by the Hornets, then Eddie said to Zeke: "Nature has plants and animals working as a team. Plants help animals and animals help plants."

Zeke looked at Eddie and said: "Uncle Eddie are you tricking me. How can animals and plants work together as a team? Is this like your question to me about a dead tree being dead?"

Eddie smiled and said: "It's called photosynthesis. Photosynthesis is a fancy word meaning: making food from sunlight." Zeke looked at Eddie and said: "Now I know that you are tricking me. Plants can't make food from sunlight; how could that happen?"

Eddie then said: "Zeke, the most important thing on Earth is water. Clean water is becoming harder to find. Humans are polluting the Earth's clean water. Water is made up of two (2) elements; Hydrogen and Oxygen. Ocean water is too salty to use; it would kill humans or plants if they needed to drink it to survive. There is a third element that plants and animals share; it's called Carbon.

Zeke looked at Eddie and said: "I'm confused. How can plants use Hydrogen, Oxygen and Carbon to make food?" Eddie looked at Zeke and said, "It is one of the amazing mysteries of Science. If you give plants water and sunlight they will make food; they will make sugar. Sugar is just those three elements mixed together. Sugar is a combination of Hydrogen, Oxygen and Carbon. Plants help animals by making sugar and they also release Oxygen into the air. Animals can't live without Oxygen. People can't live without Oxygen; we breathe in Oxygen. The animals help the plants by releasing Carbon Dioxide into the air. Plants need the Carbon Dioxide to make the fruits and vegetables that we like to eat.

It is an amazing mystery of Nature; plants and animals working together to survive and sustain life. The unsolved mystery is: 'how the sunlight' enables plants to create food (sugar) from those three (3) elements: 'Hydrogen, Oxygen, and Carbon.' There are many unsolved mysteries, but Nature has an answer or a solution to every problem. The sun is a catalyst. Zeke, you are a catalyst too."

Zeke looked at Eddie and said, "Uncle Eddie, you talk like Mr. Hill. I have no idea what you are talking about. I don't know what a catalyst is but you have the prettiest lawn in town and you grow the biggest cucumbers."

Eddie looked at Zeke and said, "A catalyst is an enabler; it allows or enables things to happen. The plants can't make food without sunlight or light energy. You are a catalyst because you enable things to happen; you help and enable Nature; you help those who need help; you are kind and caring. You enable good things to happen. You are like sunshine; you brighten people's day - just by your presence. Mr. Henry is a catalyst; he enables this town to thrive. This neighborhood wouldn't grow and thrive without humans like Mr. Henry.

My wife Edna has several friends who are catalysts; they make the lives of others better. One of Edna's friends is named Monica. Monica is a catalyst; she brings food to a food pantry. Monica buys food and donates it to people who don't have enough money to buy food.   Edna has another friend who has a Maine Coon cat. This woman and her cat are catalysts. One day I'll have you meet Carol and her cat named Chloe.

Zeke, do you remember the Gardening poem that I told you?" Zeke looked at Eddie and said, "No, I don't remember it but I would love to meet Carol's cat Chloe. Animals like me and I like animals."

Eddie looked at Zeke and said, "Gardeners know how to make things grow. Gardeners know how to reap and sow. Good gardeners sow 'kindness' and the 'reap' an abundant crop of 'joy.' Good gardeners are catalysts; they make everyone's life better. Gardeners are Nature lovers and are like sunshine; they make every day brighter. Zeke, you and Billy are catalysts --- you make people's lives better. Just keep being the nice little boy that you are and keep enjoying Nature. Nature will show you all of its treasures and I know that you will teach others how to see all of Nature's beauty."

****

*Kind and caring people truly are 'catalysts;' they enrich the lives of all who they touch. Kind and caring people are like the sun; they make other people's lives sweeter & brighter. Be a positive catalyst in someone's life.

17. Chloe the Hospice Cat

That night when Zeke went to bed, he knew that he would be dreaming about cats and catalysts. Zeke had no idea what 'photosynthesis' was. But Zeke was excited about seeing Edna's friend's cat. There were cats in Zeke's neighborhood but nobody had a Maine Coon cat. Zeke was sure that Chloe was a beautiful cat and Zeke couldn't wait to meet her. Zeke loved to pet Charlie (Mr. Hill's dog). Mr. Hill told Zeke that Charlie could sense that Zeke was special; that's why Charlie got excited every time he saw Zeke. Zeke believed that Chole would sense that Zeke was special. Zeke loved animals and was able to talk to them; he couldn't wait to pet and talk to Chloe.

The next morning after eating breakfast, Zeke went to Billy's house; he wanted to play with Billy but he wasn't home. As Zeke was walking back to his house he heard Uncle Eddie calling him. Eddie said, "Zeke, Edna's friend is here visiting. Would you like to meet her cat?" Zeke instantly responded, "Yeah! I'm coming."

Zeke ran to Uncle Eddie's house and saw this big beautiful cat. Zeke instantly said, "Uncle Eddie, I've never seen a cat this big or this pretty!" Eddie told Zeke that Chloe's owner would be back in a few minutes.

As soon as Chloe saw Zeke, she came over to him. Zeke began meowing and purring at Chloe. Chloe rubbed up against Zeke's leg then hopped onto his lap. Eddie looked at Zeke and said, "Chloe likes you. She visits us often but I've never seen her jump onto anyone's lap before."

Zeke looked at Eddie and said, "Uncle Eddie, I can talk to animals. Animals know what I'm thinking and saying. Mr. Hill said that his dog could sense that I'm special. Chloe can sense that I am special, too." Eddie looked at Zeke and said, "Maybe Mr. Hill is right (about animals sensing that you are special)."

Zeke petted and talked to Chloe for several minutes. Chloe just sat on Zeke's lap and purred. Chloe didn't even leave Zeke's lap when her owner returned. Zeke looked up when he heard someone say, "Chloe, aren't you going to come over and greet me? Don't you miss me?"

Edna (Eddie's wife) then said, "Zeke, this is my friend Carol. You are petting her cat Chloe. Carol and Chloe are volunteers at a Hospice Center. Chloe and Carol help people; they help people who are very sick. Chloe is a therapy cat."

Zeke looked at Carol then said, "That's nice that you and Chloe are helping people who are sick. Your name sounds kinda like Coral. Coral is a nurse and she has a pet mouse; it's name is Mitzi. Coral takes care of very sick children in a hospital. She lets the sick children play with her pet mouse. Mitzi (the mouse) makes the sick children feel better. Coral also gives the sick children healing pearl necklaces. Mr. Ben makes special healing pearl necklaces. Do the sick people in the Hostage Center like Chloe? Does Chloe let them pet her? Do they talk to Chloe? I know how to talk to animals. Mr. Hill said that I am special and that Nature will lead me to treasures. Would you like to see some of my treasures?"

Ms. Carol was smiling as Little Zeke was questioning her and telling her about Coral and her pet mouse. Ms. Carol had a big grin on her face as she thought about Zeke saying the phrase 'Hostage Center.' Carol looked at Zeke and said, "You are very inquisitive and Chloe sure does like you. I volunteer in a 'Hospice Center' not a Hostage Center. Most of the people in the Hospice Center love to spend time with Chloe, but some people are allergic to cats. Those people who love animals, love to pet and talk to Chloe. Chloe was trained to be calm and let strangers pet her. Chloe makes the very sick people feel better."

Zeke looked at Ms. Carol and said, "Chloe is just like Nurse Coral's pet mouse. Mitzi (the pet mouse) makes all of the sick children feel better. Uncle Eddie told me that Edna's friend Kathy called the 'Old People's Centers:' Hostage Centers. She said that some families put their old relatives in Nursing Homes, but Kathy said that they really are 'Hostage Centers' because the old people never get out of those homes.   Do the people you visit get better and get out of your Hospice Center?"

Carol looked at Zeke and said, "No, they don't get better. Hospice Centers are places where sick people receive palliative care." Zeke looked at Ms. Carol then said, "Does that mean that you and Chloe are their pals? Billy and I are pals; we're best friends. So are you and Chloe pals to the very sick people?"

Carol smiled then said, "Zeke, you are a good listener and funny too. In an unusual way, Chloe and I are pals to the very sick. We aid and help the sick people and their family members."

Zeke looked at Carol then said, "I like to aid and help people and Nature. I rescued a Box turtle twice and I rescued a bully. The bully stole my candy on Halloween night. I helped him get down from a tree, because it was the right thing to do. The Box turtle led me to a treasure."

Carol looked at Zeke and said, "That's wonderful that you are aiding Nature and people who need help. I was bullied when I was little. Groups of girls bullied me. I know how it feels to be bullied."

Zeke looked at Carol then said, "Mr. Hill said that many bullies are 'fear biters.' Coral said that she had a dog that was a fear biter. Ms. Carol, were you bullied because you have different colored eyes? Your one eye is brown and blue, it has two colors. The boy that I rescued from the tree had a birthmark on his face. He said that people make fun of his birthmark and that no one wants to be his friend. Billy's Uncle is going to try to get him to join the Boy Scouts."

Carol looked at Zeke then said, "You're very observant. The brown section of my one eye is called a 'rust spot.' I'm not sure why girls bullied me when I was little; maybe it was because I was shy and quiet. I was very tall and skinny; I just didn't fit in. I wasn't comfortable in large groups, so I got picked on."

Zeke looked at Carol then said, "That's sad that you were bullied. I'm very shy and sometimes girls look at me or point their finger at me. Girls do that to make me turn 'bright red.' I hate turning red; it's called blushing. Ms. Carol, does it bother you to have a rusty eye; will your eye rust away? Things that rust fall apart. Is your one eye going to fall out?"

Carol looked at Zeke and laughed; then she said: "My eyes are fine. I just have one eye that has two colors; it's my uniqueness." Zeke responded, "My mom said that my being quiet and shy is my uniqueness. My mom said that every child is special and has a gift to share. You and Chloe are kind and caring to sick people, so you are sharing your unique gift with sick people - just like Nurse Coral does. You are a lot like Coral. Do you like Nature?"

Carol looked at Zeke and said, "I do like Nature. I like to walk on the beach or in the mountains. Being outdoors makes me feel good. I also love to garden." Zeke looked at Carol then said, "Do you grow cucumbers? Mrs. Edna makes delicious pickles from Uncle Eddie's cucumbers."

Carol looked at Zeke then said, "I don't grow many vegetables. I love to grow flowers and have an herb garden. I don't make pickles but I do make Pesto; I use the Basil from my herb garden to make Pesto." Zeke then said, "Pesto? Isn't that what Magicians say before they do magic tricks? I don't know what Pesto is. My cranky neighbor gives my mom Rhubarb and she makes Rhubarb pie but I don't like it. I like Nature and I can see beauty in tiny little things. Can you see beauty in tiny little things?"

Carol looked at Zeke and laughed (when Zeke talked about Pesto being a Magician's word) then said, "Yes, I can see beauty in tiny little things. I see it in the sunset; I smell it in my flowers; I hear it when birds sing. Every time that I'm outdoors or with friends I can see all that is beautiful. I see beauty in you. Your kind and curious nature is absolutely beautiful."

Zeke then said, "Ms. Carol, you must be an Omegan if you like Nature and can see beauty in tiny little things. All Omegans like Nature and helping others. Mr. Hill, Mr. Ben, Nurse Coral and Uncle Eddie are Omegans. I'm an Omegan and Nature keeps showing me her treasures. You also must be a catalyst. Uncle Eddie said that catalysts make the world better and they make life brighter and sweeter. He said we are like sunshine; we brighten people's days. You are a catalyst with a cat; that's kinda funny. Your name has the same letters as Coral and catalyst has the word cat in it. Thanks for listening to me and letting me spend time with Chloe. Chloe is really nice. I like her as much as I like Mr. Hill's dog; his dog's name is Charlie. My brother said that Charlie is mean and vicious. Charlie is really nice and gets excited whenever he sees me. One day I'll show you some of my treasures. Thanks for volunteering and being nice to the sick people in the Hospice Center. Everyone likes to be around nice people. Edna is lucky to have a nice friend like you. I'm lucky that Billy is my friend. Bye!"

******

*Hospice volunteers are special. Volunteers who provide palliative care fill an important role. To die alone must be horrible. To approach one's final days surrounded by 'kind and caring' people is wonderful. I know that Chloe is bringing comfort and solace to all that she meets in the Hospice Center. Chloe is in her second year as a 'Hospice therapy cat, (as I write this). Chloe spent a weekend at my house before she became a therapy cat. Chloe and I talked a great deal that weekend. I meowed a lot and she meowed back to me. I knew that she would be a great therapy cat and she is. Chloe is purr-fect! I hope that she has many more years of aiding those in Hospice Centers.
**Pets are an example of 'pure love.' All owners feel better when they are with their pets.

After spending time with Chloe, Zeke knew that he would be dreaming about cats and in particular about a cat named Chloe. The next morning, while eating breakfast, Zeke's mom said, "Zekie, Mr. Henry called last night; he's going to take you to see Ben the jeweler. Finish your breakfast, get dressed, brush your teeth then go over to Mr. Henry's house. I'll make you a sandwich, to take with you."

Zeke was so excited! He couldn't wait to see Mr. Ben. Zeke had so many questions to ask him and he wanted to show Mr. Ben his two treasures (the special mud and the egg shaped rock that had a person's face etched in it).

Zeke quickly finished his cereal then ran upstairs to his bedroom. Zeke packed his special egg and two mud pies. Zeke had a plan; he was going to give the 'special mud' to Mr. Ben. Zeke thought that Mr. Ben could use the mud to polish his pearls. Zeke thought that his special mud had 'special healing' properties. Zeke wondered if Nurse Coral could use his 'special mud;' maybe it could help the sick children get better.

Zeke ran next door (to Mr. Henry's house) and knocked on the door. Mrs. Lillian (Mr. Henry's wife) opened the door then gave Zeke a little bag of candy; then she said: "Zekie, I like Canada mints and I know you do too - enjoy these."

Zeke looked at Mrs. Lillian then said, "Thanks Mrs. Lillian; you and Mr. Henry are my favorite neighbors - you both are so nice. Uncle Eddie said that Mr. Henry is a catalyst - he is like 'sunshine;' he brightens everyone's day. Mrs. Lillian, you are a catalyst too. You brighten everyone's day too; you are like 'sunshine' and I like your Canada mints. I like the pink mints the best. Thanks for the candy." Mrs. Lillian just smiled at Zeke's comments.

As soon as Henry and Zeke got into Henry's car, Henry said: "Zeke I have a present for you." Then Henry handed Zeke a paper bag. Zeke was so excited and said, "Mr. Henry, can I look and see what's in the bag or do I have to wait until Christmas?" Henry smiled (at Zeke's excitement and response), then said: "You don't have to wait until Christmas; open it now."

Zeke opened the paper bag and was amazed at what he saw. Inside the bag was a 'velvet bag.' The velvet bag had letters on it; the letters 'J.E.D.' were on it. Zeke opened the velvet bag and found three (3) things: there was a large marble, a fossilized rock, and a blue bottle. Zeke held each item in his hand; he knew that each was a treasure. Zeke then said to Mr. Henry, "Mr. Henry, where did you find these treasures? Did Nature lead you to its treasures? Nature leads me to treasures."

Henry looked at Zeke then said, "Nature doesn't lead me to treasures, but I'm in the burial business; I dig graves. Sometimes when I'm digging a grave I find unique things. I know how you like to collect things, so I thought that you might enjoy these things. Long ago, people would bury things in their backyards. If I find things that I think are old or interesting I bring them home. Mrs. Lillian likes me bringing her flowers but she doesn't want me bringing her buried items like these. Zeke, you see these things as treasures but Lil would say that they are junk."

Zeke looked at Mr. Henry then said, "These are treasures! I know when I see or find a treasure. I am special and have a gift; I can see beauty - in 'tiny little things;' these are beautiful and they are treasures! Thanks so much, Mr. Henry! You are my favorite neighbor and Uncle Eddie said that you are a catalyst." Henry smiled and laughed as Zeke was talking, then he thought: 'this little boy is so 'pure & innocent' --- I hope that he stays that way.'

It was a thirty minute ride to Ben's jewelry store so Zeke ate some of Mrs. Lillian's candy and studied his gifts (i.e., treasures from Henry). As Zeke looked at the large marble he noticed that letters and words could be seen inside of the marble as he shook it and turned it. Zeke wondered if it was like a 'magic 8-ball;' some teenagers had 'magic balls' that they said could answer questions --- they said the balls were like fortune tellers. When Zeke looked at the rock, he could see a skeleton in the rock. He said to Henry, "Mr. Henry, I can see an animal's skeleton in this rock; this must be a fossil of an ancient animal; maybe it's a dinosaur fossil." Henry responded, "Maybe it is."

Then Zeke looked carefully at the third treasure (the bottle). The bottle was a small blue bottle. As Zeke put the bottle close to his face, he heard a sound. Zeke was sure that the bottle was talking, so Zeke put the bottle up to his ear. When Zeke placed the neck of the bottle next to his ear he could hear a 'whistling sound;' this made Zeke think of his friends 'blowing into empty soda bottles.' All of Zeke's friends would blow into soda bottles and make them whistle. Zeke also noticed that the bottle had numbers and letters on the bottom of it; this made Zeke think that those letters and numbers were a code. Zeke looked at Henry then said: "These really are treasures and I know that they will lead me to more treasures. Mr. Hill said that I am special and that Nature will lead me to its treasures. Mr. Hill l'ves near Mr. Ben's store. I would like you to meet Mr. Hill. Mr. Hill is nice like you. Mr. Henry, can we stop and see Mr. Hill after we leave Mr. Ben's store?" Henry responded, "Sure, we can stop and see Mr. Hill."

As soon as Henry and Zeke walked into Ben's store, Ben said: "Henry, it's great to see you! I hope Lillian is enjoying her pearl necklace. I see that you brought one of my special 'little friends.' I didn't know that you knew 'Little Zeke.' Little Zeke is Ideal's nephew." Henry looked at Ben then said: "Zeke is my next door neighbor. Zeke's dad and I are very good friends. Lil loves her necklace but I want you to put a new clasp on it."

Zeke looked at Ben then said: "Mr. Ben, I have a lot of questions for you. I've been finding treasures in my hometown. Maya, your 'special pigeon,' brought me a note and led me to an 'egg-shaped' rock. I want you to look at the egg-shaped rock that

I found in a birdhouse. Maya led me to the birdhouse. This rock has a person's face etched into it. Maya landed on my shoulder and when I opened her leg band it had a note in it; the note said: 'the log cabin is gone and Sandy was sad.' Mr. Ben, is Sandy okay; what happened to the log cabin?"

Ben looked at Zeke then said: "Sandy is fine. A fisherman named Ray saw her lying on the beach one day. Sandy was looking towards the log cabin house's site; but the log cabin was torn down. The owners died and their children sold the property. The new owners wanted a 'modern looking house.' So if you go to the inlet jetty you will see a large mansion where the log cabin used to be; they call that progress. Nobody wants to keep the old historic homes; when Mr. Hill dies someone will tear down his house and build a modern day mansion in its place.

When the fisherman saw Sandy lying motionless on the beach, he called the Marine Mammal Stranding Center. The volunteers, from the 'Stranding Center,' came and rescued Sandy. Veterinarians checked Sandy and found that she was healthy; she was just very sad. The 'Stranding Center' released Sandy back into the ocean. We are lucky to have 'The Marine Mammal Stranding Center' nearby; they rescue all types of ocean life. Sometimes they care for sea turtles that are injured and sometimes they aid whales. Sea turtles are often tangled in fishing lines & fishing nets; they also can be sickened from swallowing plastic bags. Turtles like to eat jellyfish and sometimes they eat plastic bags (they think the bags are jellyfish)."

Zeke looked at Ben then said: "Mr. Ben, when you fix Mr. Henry's pearl necklace would put your 'special silky string' on it. It will last forever if you put your special string on it. Mr. Henry is my favorite neighbor. Uncle Eddie said that Mr. Henry is a positive catalyst. Mr. Henry makes good things happen in my town. Mr. Henry is 'kind and aids' everyone. He is kind to 'Italians' like my dad, and he is kind to Hispanics, African Americans, Jewish, Irish --- Mr. Henry is the 'sunshine' of our town; he makes everyone's life 'brighter & sweeter.' My dad isn't an 'invasive species' to Mr. Henry. My dad is a good friend. Mr. Ben, I want you to look at my egg-shaped rock; it's special."

Ben smiled and laughed as Zeke talked about Henry and Italians being an invasive species, then Ben said: "Let me see your special egg-shaped rock." As soon as Ben looked at it he saw the profile of a woman's face and said: "Zeke, I've seen one other rock like this. I want you to show this rock to Mr. Hill. I think that he can tell you about this rock. Stop and see Mr. Hill." Zeke responded, "We are going to stop and see Mr. Hill. I want Mr. Henry to meet Mr. Hill."

Zeke then took out two plastic bags and said: "Mr. Ben, I want you to have some of my 'special mud.' My mud has 'healing powers;' it healed the cuts that were on my hands and it makes my hands feel 'warm & tingly.' Maybe Nurse Coral could use it to help the sick children who are in the hospital." Ben then looked at Zeke and said: "Thanks for the 'special mud;' I'll tell Coral about it and let you know what she says."

Zeke looked at Henry then said, "Mr. Henry, we can go and see Mr. Hill while Mr. Ben is repairing Mrs. Lillian's necklace." Henry looked at Zeke and said, "OK, that's a good idea. Ben I'll be back later; I know that Zeke wants to spend some time with Mr. Hill."

When Zeke and Henry pulled up to Mr. Hill's house, he was sitting on his porch reading; his dog Charlie was lying next to him. As soon as Zeke got out of Henry's car, Charlie started to wag his tail. Charlie's tail was wagging 'super fast;' he was so happy to see Zeke. Zeke looked at Charlie and said, "Hi Charlie, Hi Mr. Hill. Charlie remembers me; his tail is wagging 'super fast.' Mr. Hill, I want you to meet my favorite neighbor. Mr. Hill, this is Mr. Henry; he knows Mr. Ben too. Mr. Henry is the 'sunshine' of our town --- he's the nicest man."

Henry was smiling as Zeke talked so 'glowingly' about him, then Henry said: "Mr. Hill, Zeke really likes you and thinks that you are special. He told me a lot about you and your house. He told me how much you love your house and this barrier island. It's a pleasure to meet you."

Mr. Hill looked at Henry and said, "You can call me Dan. It's a pleasure to meet you. I can see that Zeke really likes you. Zeke is a 'special' little boy and he's very insightful. He's a very 'kind & caring' little boy."

Zeke took out his egg shaped rock and said, "Mr. Hill, I found this treasure in the woods. Mr. Ben's 'special pigeon,' named Maya, led me to this treasure. Mr. Ben said that I should show it to you. He said that you could tell me about it." As soon as Mr. Hill looked at Zeke's rock, he walked out of the room. Zeke had no idea why he walked away.

Then Mr. Hill walked back into the room; he was holding something in his hand. He opened his hand and showed Zeke an 'egg-shaped' rock. Mr. Hill's rock looked just like Zeke's rock. Zeke looked at Mr. Hill's rock, then said: "Where did you find your treasure; was your egg-shaped rock in a birdhouse?"

Mr. Hill looked at Zeke then said: "I found my egg-shaped rock on Bessie Hill's tombstone. I went to visit her grave one day and this egg-shaped rock was lying on top of her tombstone." Then Mr. Hill opened his other hand and showed Zeke a locket. The locket was beautiful and opened. When Mr. Hill opened the locket, there was a picture of a woman. Mr. Hill then said, "This is a picture of Bessie Hill. The woman's face that is etched into your rock and mine is the profile of Bessie Hill.

Bessie died suddenly. She was only 37 years old when she was found dead. Her sudden death is still a mystery. Bessie had two children. When Bessie died her children became orphans. Her two children were separated; one child was raised by one of Bessie's siblings and her oldest child was raised by her niece; her niece's name was Coral. Bessie was the 11th child in her family and her name was Elizabeth. Bessie's oldest daughter was named Ruth but was often called Mitzi.

I've never been able to find out how Bessie died. Her death certificate listed her cause of death as: 'asphyxiation.' Bessie is buried next to her mother and father. I was named after her father. Little Zeke, I think that you will solve the mystery of Bessie's sudden death. I know that you are special and I know that Nature is leading you to treasures. I now know that you and I are somehow connected, but I don't know how we are connected."

Zeke looked at Mr. Hill, then said: "Wow! That's an amazing story. I can't believe that you and I have 'identical' egg-shaped rocks. Uncle Eddie said that there are a lot of mysteries in Nature and in life. He said that Nature has the answer to every mystery and every problem. I'm sure that Nature will lead me to the answer - (of the cause Bessie's death). Mr. Hill, I knew that you were special; I now know that Nature leads you to treasures too." Then Zeke started petting and rubbing Charlie's back.

Henry and Mr. Hill sat on the porch and talked. While they were talking, Zeke was enjoying 'petting & rubbing' Charlie. After fifteen minutes, Zeke asked Mr. Hill if he could take Charlie for a walk. Zeke said, "Mr. Hill, can I walk Charlie to the inlet jetty? I want to see the new home that was built where the old log cabin was."

Mr. Hill looked at Zeke then said, "Sure you can take Charlie for a walk. He loves to walk on the beach. I see that someone told you about the log cabin being torn down, but do you know about the seal and her connection to the log cabin?"

Zeke looked at Mr. Hill then said, "No, was the seal owned by the people who lived in the log cabin? Mr. Hill then said, "The people who lived in the log cabin didn't own the seal but they always left the basement window open (for the seal). The seal would occasionally walk up the beach and go into their basement. So the people had a little wading pool in their basement - just for the seal. If they heard splashing in their basement pool they would feed the seal some fresh fish. The seal became part of the lore of this island. The seal became famous like 'Marty & Murray.' Some islanders called the seal 'Sandy;' some called her 'Ci-Ci' (the sea's seal). I called her Sandy."

Zeke then said to Mr. Hill, "I didn't know that Sandy would live in the basement of the log cabin. One time when I was swimming in the ocean she swam by me 'super fast' and scared me. I didn't know what it was. Then she swam next to me and poked her head out of the water. I smiled when I saw her looking at me, and she smiled (back at me) then swam away."

Mr. Hill then said, "Sandy would stay at that log cabin for a few days then go out to sea for months; then she would come back to that house and stay for a few more days. The islanders knew that Sandy used that house as a resting place. Sandy (the seal) knew that the log cabin and the people who lived there were Nature lovers; that log cabin was a 'safe haven' for her. Sandy no longer has that home as a safe haven, but she was rescued and is well."

When Zeke got to the jetty with Charlie, he stopped and stared at the big mansion that now stood where the log cabin was. While staring at the big house he heard a man say: "Hi Little boy, do you remember me? I'm the fisherman who always carried a bird cage; I always had my parakeet named Anita with me. I saw you staring at that house. The log cabin was torn down but Sandy, the seal, is fine."

Zeke looked at the man then said: "Hi Mr. Man! How is Anita? Did her feathers grow back?" The man looked at Zeke then said, "No, her feathers didn't grow back. She died two days after I last saw you. I was sad for a long time. My name is Ray. You can call me Ray.

One day I saw Sandy (the seal) lying on the beach; she was looking for the log cabin but it had been torn down. Sandy (the seal) just laid on the beach sand; she didn't move. I could tell that she was sad, so I called the Marine Mammal Stranding Center. Volunteers from the Center came and took Sandy. They kept Sandy at the Marine Mammal Center for a few days and saw that she was healthy so they released her back into the ocean. I'm happy that Sandy is well and I'm happy that we have Marine Mammal Stranding Centers."

Zeke looked at the man then said, "I'm so sorry to hear about your parakeet named Anita; I know how much you loved your pet. I love my parakeet very much. That was very nice of you to rescue Sandy; you are an Omegan like me. All Omegans love Nature. Your name is a good name for an Omega; you are a 'ray of sunshine' --- you made Sandy's life better. Uncle Eddie would say that you are a 'positive catalyst;' you make the world a better place. Thanks for stopping to talk to me and for rescuing Sandy. If you are ever feeling sad you can come and spend time with my parakeet. My parakeet will sing to you. Bye, Mr. Ray. I have to walk Charlie back home. My neighbor has to give me a ride home."

When Zeke got back to Mr. Hill's house with Charlie, Mr. Henry said: "Mr. Hill and I had a wonderful conversation but Zeke we have to leave now." Zeke then said, "OK, Mr. Henry. Bye Mr. Hill, I'm glad that you got to meet Mr. Henry; he's my favorite neighbor. Bye Charlie!"

On the ride home, Henry handed Zeke a piece of chipped siding and said: "Zeke, do you know what this is?" Zeke looked at it and said, "It looks like a broken piece of Mr. Hill's house." Henry looked at Zeke and said, "That's what it is and I have a plan. I'm going to bring a crew of workers to Mr. Hill's house; we're going to repair and paint the outside, and we're going to put a new roof on his house. Mr. Hill truly is a nice man and I can see why you like him so much."

Zeke looked at Mr. Henry then said, "Mr. Henry, that's really nice of you. You really do add sunshine to the world; you are a 'ray of light.' I know that Mr. Hill will be surprised but very happy. I want to come with you when you bring your crew of workers;

I can play with Charlie - while you work on Mr. Hill's house. Thanks for bringing me to see Mr. Ben and Mr. Hill; you're the best neighbor --- in the whole world."

****

19. Dexter - the Rabbit

After visiting Mr. Ben and Mr. Hill, Zeke's mind was racing. So many things were going through his mind. Zeke couldn't believe that there were two 'identical' egg-shaped rocks. He also kept thinking about the mystery of a woman's sudden death. Zeke was sure that Nature would lead him to more treasures and Zeke was sure that Nature would help him learn more about Bessie Hill's death.

Zeke had another wonderful day, but the walk on the beach made him very sleepy. As soon as Zeke hopped onto his bed he heard a noise coming from downstairs. Zeke heard his brother yelling, "Zeke! Did the monsters get you? Answer me!" Every night was the same. Zeke went to bed first, because he was the youngest child and Zack waited downstairs.

Zeke believed that Zack wanted him to be eaten by the monsters that they thought were under their beds. Zack didn't know that Zeke (his little brother) wasn't afraid of monsters (any more). Zeke learned that there weren't any monsters living under his bed, but Zeke let Zack continue believing that monsters lived under their beds. Zeke enjoyed being 'braver' than his older brother.

Tonight, Zeke didn't respond to Zack. Zeke was thinking about Bessie Hill, two identical egg-shaped rocks, Sandy (the seal), and Anita (the featherless parakeet). Zeke felt sad because Mr. Ray told him that his pet parakeet, named Anita, had died. Zeke knew that he would be dreaming about animals and unsolved mysteries.

When Zeke awoke the next morning his brother (Zack) yelled, "Zeke! Go out back and look at the rabbit cage. Mrs. Lucia's cat killed my Easter bunny and your bunny is missing. I saw Mrs. Lucia's cat in the alley and I shot it with one of my arrows. I didn't kill it but I 'nicked' it. It ran away, but if I see it, in our yard again, I'm going to shoot it with my bow & arrows."

Zeke quickly ran outside (to the rabbit cage) and saw Zack's dead bunny. Zeke felt sad (for Zack and the bunny). Then Zeke looked at Zack and said: "That's horrible that your bunny got killed but you shouldn't shoot Mrs. Lucia's cat. Mrs. Lucia would be very sad if her cat was killed; she loves her cat. How do you know that it was Mrs. Lucia's cat that killed your bunny? Did you see it?" Zack responded, "No, I didn't see it but cats are predators and they kill mice; so I'm sure that it was her cat."

Zeke began looking all over his backyard for his little bunny. Zack and Zeke's parents gave them each a bunny as an Easter present. Several of Zeke's friends were given bunnies as Easter presents. Zeke was unable to find his bunny anywhere in his yard, so he went back to the rabbit cage. While looking at the rabbits' cage he noticed that the chicken wire fencing was not attached in one corner. Zeke looked at Zack and said, "I guess we didn't nail all of the rabbit cage fencing, it's not attached in this one corner. The predator animal probably got into the cage where we didn't attach this corner fence wire." Zack responded, "It wasn't me. It must have been the corner that you nailed. I know that Mrs. Lucia's cat killed my bunny! I'm so mad, I'm going to make that cat pay."

Zeke looked at Zack and thought: 'Zack sure has a temper. He gets so mad. He's super mean when he loses his temper and gets mad.' Then Zeke said: "Zack, I'll help you bury your bunny. We'll bury your bunny in the back corner of our yard and I'll put a wooden cross by the bunny's grave."

After burying Zack's bunny, Zeke went inside and ate his breakfast. When Zeke finished his breakfast he decided to look for his bunny. Zeke's bunny wasn't in the cage with Zack's. Zeke thought that his bunny might have escaped the predator.

While Zeke was looking for his bunny he smelled an unusual scent. There was a 'lavender' scent coming from the edge of Zeke's yard. When Zeke walked to that side of his backyard all he saw were Lilac bushes. Zeke's dad had planted beautiful purple Lilac bushes. The lilac flowers were just beginning to bloom. Zeke loved the smell of Lilacs.

Zeke knew that the 'lavender' scent was coming from where the Lilac bushes were. Zeke was confused and thought: 'I know the smell of lavender. This lavender scent is coming from my dad's Lilac bushes.' Zeke decided to look under the Lilac bushes.

Zeke was amazed at what he found. Underneath the Lilac bushes was a pile of leaves. Zeke carefully moved the leaves and saw a 'burrow' --- there was a tunnel leading under the ground. Zeke bent down and looked closely into the tunnel. He knew that the lavender smell was coming out of the tunnel. Zeke's mind was racing; his mind was often racing and thinking about discovering treasures. So Zeke moved away from the tunnel and closed his eyes. He took three (3) deep breaths and opened his eyes. As soon as Zeke opened his eyes he saw a bunny rabbit looking at him.

Zeke couldn't believe his eyes. At the entrance to the underground tunnel was a rabbit. The rabbit was looking at Zeke and the rabbit smelled like 'lavender.' The rabbit that was looking at Zeke wasn't Zeke's Easter bunny (the present that his parents had given him). Zeke's mind instantly said: "Zeke, you are special. Animals know what you are thinking. You can talk to animals."

So Zeke looked at the rabbit and said: "Hi Mr. Rabbit. Do you know where my bunny is? My brother, (Zack), thinks that a predator killed both of our bunnies, but my bunny isn't in the cage. Is my bunny alive?" The rabbit looked at Zeke and nodded (with his head). Zeke looked at the rabbit then said: "Mr. Rabbit, you just nodded that my bunny is alive. Do you know where my bunny is?" The rabbit looked at Zeke and nodded again.

Now Zeke began smiling at the rabbit because he was happy. Zeke was happy that his bunny was alive. While Zeke was smiling he noticed that the rabbit smiled back at him. Zeke then said: "Mr. Rabbit, are you smiling at me?" The rabbit looked at Zeke, then smiled, winked and nodded.

Zeke couldn't believe his eyes. He couldn't believe that a rabbit could smile and wink or that a rabbit could nod. But Zeke believed that he could communicate with animals. Then Zeke said, "Mr. Rabbit, did you rescue my bunny? Did you save my bunny from the predator?" The Rabbit looked at Zeke then said, "Yes, I did rescue your bunny. Your rabbit ran out of the cage when the predator got into the cage. I led your bunny to my tunnel. My name is Dexter, but you can call me Dex. I know that you are a Nature lover and are always kind to animals and to everyone. I have much to tell you and teach you. Today I want you to know that your bunny is fine but I must teach him how to survive in the wild. It will take some time for me to 'imprint' and teach survival skills to your bunny.

Rabbits shouldn't be Easter presents. Rabbits should be enjoyed in their natural habitat. I am called Dexter because I am 'ambidextrous.' I can throw and catch with either hand (paw). One day when your friend Billy isn't home you can throw me your best pitches and I will show you how talented I am. Today, I want you to know that your bunny is fine. I want you to know that a 'rabbit's foot' keychain isn't a good luck charm. The necklace that you always wear is a good luck charm. Zeke, I will always be hare (here) for you." The rabbit then looked at Zeke and: 'smiled, winked and nodded;' then the rabbit disappeared into the tunnel.

A few seconds later the rabbit came out of the tunnel again. The rabbit was wearing a hat. Dexter, (the rabbit), ran up to Zeke then jerked his head. When Dexter 'jerked' his head, the hat that he was wearing fell on the ground in front of Zeke. Dexter looked at Zeke then said: "You'll know what to do with this hat." Then Dexter looked at Zeke and: 'smiled, winked and nodded.' Before Zeke could respond, Dexter turned and ran back into his tunnel.

Zeke just sat on the ground and thought about what the rabbit had just said to him. So many thoughts were racing through Zeke's mind. Zeke picked up the hat (that Dexter had just given to him). As Zeke looked at the hat he saw the letters: 'BtB' on the hat. Zeke knew that this was 'Bruiser's hat.' Zeke knew what he should do with the hat, but the hat was dirty.

Zeke knew that he had to tell Uncle Eddie or Mr. Hill about this rabbit. Zeke knew that he couldn't tell his brother Zack. He knew that Zack would say that Zeke made it up. Zack always said that Zeke was a storyteller. Zeke knew what he saw, so

he quickly put the leaves back over the rabbit's tunnel and walked down to tell Uncle
Eddie.

****

20. The Caterpillar and the Man

When Zeke got to Uncle Eddie's he saw Eddie working in his garden. Zeke
yelled, "Uncle Eddie, you won't believe what just happened to me." Eddie responded,
"Have a seat on my porch; I'll bring out a popsicle. You can tell me what happened,
while you are eating your popsicle."

Zeke told Eddie all about his recent trip to Mr. Ben's, and Mr. Hill's. He also told
him about Sandy (the seal) and Mr. Ray. Zeke also told Eddie that Mr. Henry was going
to bring a crew of workers to repair Mr.Hill's house.

Eddie felt bad when Zeke told him about a predator killing Zack's bunny. Eddie
also felt bad about Zack shooting Mrs. Lucia's cat with an arrow. When Eddie heard
Zeke tell him about a 'lavender smelling rabbit' named Dexter he said: "Giuseppe had a
pet rabbit that smelled like lavender. Giuseppe's rabbit was named Esperanto. People
would say that Giuseppe could talk to his rabbit and that his rabbit could smile, wink and
nod."

Zeke looked at Eddie and said, "This rabbit smiled, winked and nodded at me,
too. This rabbit said that his name was 'Dexter;' he said that he was 'ambidextrous.'
Dexter said that he rescued my rabbit and that he had to 'imprint' or teach my rabbit
how to survive in the wild. Dexter said that 'rabbit's foot' keychains aren't lucky. Before
running into his tunnel, he said: "I am hare (here) for you. Uncle Eddie, are rabbit's foot
keychains good luck charms?"

Eddie looked at Zeke, then said: "No, rabbit's foot keychains aren't good luck
charms; that's another myth. It sure is not lucky for the rabbit. Killing a rabbit then
putting its feet on keychains doesn't bring anyone luck."

Then Eddie began telling Zeke about another legend. Eddie said: "Zeke, it may
not have been Mrs. Lucia's cat that killed Zack's bunny. It might have been a fox or a
coyote. There is a legend in this town about Franny the fox and about Kernie's
Coyotes.

You know that there is a kids' prison in our town; it's near the creek where you
like to explore. The prison is called a 'Detention Home.' Kids who run away from home
or kids who 'get into trouble' - (break the law and get arrested), are put into the
Detention Home. The Superintendent of the Detention Home tells the children (who are
arrested and placed into his Detention Home) that there are Foxes and Coyotes in the
woods around the Detention Home. The Children are told this legend so that they don't

try to 'escape' from the Detention Home. At night you can hear the sound of Wolves howling. Most of the kids who are in the Detention Home are afraid of the Superintendent and of the Coyotes."

Zeke looked at Eddie then said: "I heard about Franny the Fox and about the Coyotes; are there really Coyotes and Foxes in the woods by the creek?" Eddie looked at Zeke and said: "There are Coyotes and Foxes in the woods around here, and they might have killed Zack's bunny; but you won't hear them howling. The howling sounds are the sounds of Wolves howling in the night. The Superintendent plays 'howling wolves' sounds over a 'loudspeaker;' he does this to frighten the kids. He doesn't want any kids to escape at night (when he's sleeping)."

Zeke looked at Eddie then said: "That's sad for the kids who are locked up in the 'Detention Home;' they must be sad. I know that I would be sad if I were locked up and I would be super scared if I heard Coyotes howling."

Eddie looked at Zeke then said: "It is sad to see any child locked up. Zeke, you are lucky. You have nice parents and live in a nice neighborhood. Some children have mean parents and some are abused. Some children run away from their homes."

Then Zeke looked at Eddie and said: "Uncle Eddie, look at what the 'lavender' smelling rabbit gave me. Dexter, (the rabbit), gave me this hat. I know that it's Bruiser's hat. The hat has the letters: 'BtB' on it. I'm going to give the hat back to Bruiser, but I'm going to have my mom wash it first because it's dirty.

Uncle Eddie, do you think that Bruiser could change and become a 'nice boy?' I like to help people and you said that Bruiser's dad was a 'bully.' Maybe Bruiser is a 'fear biter.' I'm going to see if Colonel Arnold will mentor him. Mr. Arnold is a friend of my dad's. My dad was Mr. Arnold's football coach when Mr. Arnold was a teenager. Mr. Arnold is an Air Force Officer and is a volunteer football coach. My dad said that he would talk to Mr. Arnold. Mr. Arnold could teach Bruiser how to play football. Bruiser would be a good football player because he's so 'big and strong.' I think that Bruiser will be happy to get his hat back."

Eddie looked at Zeke and said: "Wow! That's wonderful that you are going to give Bruiser his hat back and that your dad is going to see if he can get Bruiser on the football team. I believe that all children (who are bullies or who are bullied) can become 'kind and caring' people; if they are given: 'love and guidance' - from caring adults. I'm sure that Mr. Arnold would be able to help Bruiser. Mr. Arnold is a very nice man."
Then Eddie looked at Zeke and said: "Zeke, you really do have a 'special' connection to Nature. Nature keeps showing you treasures and teaching you. It's wonderful that you are going to try and aid Bruiser. Let me tell you a story about a man and a caterpillar. After I tell you this story, I'll ask you a question."

Zeke looked at Eddie then said, "Ok. Uncle Eddie, I like listening to your stories, but I hope that you don't ask me another trick question." Eddie smiled, then said: "Zeke,

you are very wise and insightful; you are also a very good listener. Enjoy a piece of
candy as I tell you my story about a Caterpillar and a man."

Then Eddie began telling Zeke the following story: "A man saw a caterpillar in
his garden and said: Mr. Caterpillar! Why are you eating my plant? The caterpillar
looked at the man and said: 'Because I Can.' The man looked back at the caterpillar
and said: 'Please Mr.Caterpillar, don't eat my Fennel plant. I love my Fennel plant.
Why must you eat my Fennel plant? The Caterpillar looked at the man and said:
'Because I Can.' The man looked back at the caterpillar and said: "Mr. Caterpillar, I
really want my Fennel plant to grow and blossom. I need it to blossom so that I can
have seeds. I use the seeds in my food and use them to grow more Fennel plants.
Please don't eat my Fennel plant; you're eating all of my Fennel plant. Why must you
eat all of the leaves on my Fennel plant?" The caterpillar looked at the man and said:
'Because I Can't.'

Now the man was really confused; he was scratching his head (he was
perplexed) then said: "Mr. Caterpillar, I'm really confused. First, you said that you're
eating all of my Fennel 'because you can.' Then you said that you're eating all of my
Fennel 'because you can't.' Please explain that to me; I don't understand --- you say
you can then you say you can't. Can and can't are the opposite; please help me
understand what you mean.

The caterpillar looked at the man and said: "Mr. Man, I know that you are a
Nature loving man. And I know that you love your Fennel plants. Most people would kill
me or spray poison on me, if they saw me eating their plants. Since you are a Nature
loving man and are always kind to Nature, you will understand what I mean when I say -
'I can' & 'I can't.' The caterpillar stopped chewing the Fennel stalk and said: "I'm eating
your Fennel plant because I can. I'm eating your Fennel plant because I can't. I must
eat your Fennel plant if I want to become a beautiful butterfly. I can't become a
beautiful Swallowtail Butterfly, unless I eat your plant. Fennel plants are 'host' plants for
Swallowtail Butterflies. Please let me eat your Fennel plant? Mr. Man, now do you
understand what I mean when I say 'I Can' & when I say 'I Can't?'

The man looked back at the caterpillar then said: "Mr. Caterpillar, I now
understand. Thanks for explaining to me --- why you 'Can' and why you 'Can't.' I know
that you truly don't want to make me sad or want to hurt my Fennel plant. I know that
you just want to become a beautiful butterfly. I 'can' & I 'will' let you eat my Fennel
plants. I can 'see' & I 'understand.'

You are an 'ugly' & 'scary' looking caterpillar, and it pains me to see you eat my
Fennel plant, but I know that you just want to become a beautiful butterfly. You just
want to become a beautiful 'piece of Nature.' Some humans are like you, Mr.
Caterpillar. Some humans go through a 'destructive phase' of life, before they become
a beautiful 'piece of Nature.' But some humans never develop into a beautiful 'piece of

Nature.' Keep eating my Fennel plant, then return to my yard. Please come back and let me see you as a beautiful 'Swallowtail Butterfly.' You know how much I like butterflies. I love butterflies; they help pollinate my flowers. Thanks for taking the time to explain: 'why you can;' 'why you can't;' and 'why you must.' --- eat my Fennel plants."

Zeke looked at Eddie then said: "Uncle Eddie, I have no idea what this story means. I hope your question isn't about caterpillar poop. Caterpillar poop is disgusting."

Eddie looked at Zeke, then said: "No Zeke, my question for you isn't about caterpillar poop. My question for you is this: "Is it better to live a long life and be miserable or is it better to go through a painful stage then develop into a beautiful piece of Nature?" Zeke looked at Eddie then said: "That's not a trick question, and I know the answer too. I think this story relates to 'Bruiser the bully.' Right now Bruiser is an 'ugly and scary' caterpillar but he could become a beautiful butterfly. I'm going to try and help him become a 'beautiful piece of Nature.' I like to help people who need help!"

Eddie looked at Zeke, then said: "I knew that you would understand. Zeke, you are a 'beautiful piece of Nature' and a 'positive catalyst' ---- you brighten everyone's day! Enjoy a piece of candy and watch the Monarch butterfly feed on my flowers."

****

21. Depth vs Length

After listening to Uncle Eddie's caterpillar story, Zeke knew that he would be dreaming about caterpillars and caterpillar poop. Zeke also knew that he would be thinking about a plan to aid Bruiser. Zeke believed that Bruiser was a 'fear-biter.' Zeke believed that Bruiser could become a nice person. But before falling asleep and dreaming about helping Bruiser, Zeke had to listen to the same night time sounds.

As soon as Zeke hopped onto his bed, he heard Zack yelling: "Zeke! Zeke! Did the monsters get you! Answer me!" Every night was the same. But Zeke was sure that he would awake with a plan. Zeke knew that Nature would teach him and show him: 'how to aid those in need' --- even when he was sleeping. Within a minute, Zeke was sound asleep, but Zack wasn't. Zack was scared - and reluctant to walk upstairs to bed.

The next morning, Zeke remembered his dream. After eating his breakfast, Zeke said: "Mom, did you wash Bruiser's hat?" Zeke's mom responded, "Yes I did. The hat is in the laundry room; it's on the drying rack." Then Zeke said, "Mom, I'm going to give Bruiser his hat back. You know that I like to help people and Bruiser really misses his favorite hat. I'll be back in a few minutes." Zeke's mom responded: "That's very nice of you to return his hat; I hope that he appreciates getting it back." Zeke then said: "I know that he will. Nature wanted me to aid him; that's why Dexter gave me his hat."

When Zeke knocked on Bruiser's front door, his mom answered and said: "Little boy, can I help you?" Zeke responded, "My name is Zeke. A rabbit in my yard brought me this hat. I had my mom wash it because it was dirty. I know that it's Bruiser's hat because it has the letters: 'BtB' on it. Bruiser told me that it is his favorite hat." The mom looked at Zeke then said, "That was very kind of you. It is R. J.'s favorite hat; he's been sad since he lost it." Then the mom said: "R. J. come here; there's someone here to see you."

When R. J. got to the front door, his mom walked away. R. J. looked at Zeke then said: "What do you want!?!" Zeke looked at Bruiser then said, "I found your favorite hat and I want you to have it back." Zeke handed the hat to Bruiser then said: "A special rabbit gave it to me and said that I would know what to do with it. The rabbit's name is Dexter. I had my mom wash it because it was dirty. I know how much you love your hat."

Bruiser looked at Zeke then said, "Why are you being so nice to me? No one has ever been nice to me; everyone is afraid of me." Zeke looked at Bruiser then said, "I'm nice to everyone. I like to help people. I don't think that you are a bully. I think that you are a 'fear-biter.' I think that you are just in an 'ugly caterpillar stage.' I think that you could become a 'beautiful butterfly.' You don't have to punch people in the arm and leave bruises on their arms. You could wave or give a 'high five;' instead of punching people in the arm."

Bruiser then said, "Little kid, you're talking strange. I'm not an 'ugly caterpillar.' The letters on my hat mean: <u>Bruiser the Bully</u>; that's what 'BtB' stands for. I'm the toughest kid in town. But I'm glad that you brought my hat back; I really missed it. Thanks, Little kid; I kinda like you. I'll protect you and won't take any of your candy."

Zeke looked at Bruiser then said: "See, you can be nice. You just thanked me. I don't need your protection, because Nature will protect me from all bullies. I just want you to become a 'beautiful piece of Nature.' You don't have to remain a bully, you can change. You are really strong and could be a great football player. Instead of punching people, you could become the 'best tackler' on the football team. I know that you could become a great football player. My dad was an 'All-State' football player when he was in high school. My dad coached Colonel Arnold (in football). Coach Arnold is going to call you and ask you to join his football team. I know that you could become a star football player. I hope that you join Mr. Arnold's team."

Bruiser looked at Zeke then said: "Thanks for saying that I'm really strong and that I could be a great football player. I never played football. I was always afraid to try out for the football team. When I'm nervous, I stutter. The only time that I don't stutter is when I'm mad. When I was little, my dad made fun of me everytime that I stuttered. My dad would mimic my stuttering; it just made me stutter more. Then, my dad would say, 'toughen up!' He would say that I have to be 'tougher.' He would say, 'be the toughest kid in town then no one will pick on you;' so I became a bully. I can't believe that you are trying to help me. No one has ever tried to help me."

Zeke looked at Bruiser then said: "I told you that I like to help people. I know that you could change. You could start by saying that the letters on your hat (BtB) mean: 'Be the Best.' When someone asks you what the letters on your hat mean, you can say: the letters mean: 'Be the Best.' Then you can say that you are ALWAYS trying to get better at everything that you do. You can recite the phrase: 'Good, Better, Best - Never let it rest --- until your Good is Better and your Better is Best.' Uncle Eddie told me that when I have self-doubts, (about my abilities), that I should recite the phrase: 'You are better than you think you are, but not as good as you could be.' He said that we should practice and try to get better at whatever we want to master."

Then Zeke looked at Bruiser and said: "There are people who can help you when you start stuttering. I had an uncle who stuttered when he was young. I'll ask him how he overcame his stuttering problem. Whenever I get nervous, I close my eyes and take three (3) deep breaths. When I open my eyes I am less nervous; try that. Bruiser, can I call you R.J. - instead of Bruiser?"

Bruiser looked at Zeke and said, "Sure you can call me R.J; but not in front of my peers. I don't want them to laugh at me. Thanks again, for bringing my hat back. I am going to join the football team, if Mr. Arnold calls me." Zeke then said, "You're welcome R.J; I can't wait to see you playing football. I know that you're going to be great. BYE!"

As Zeke was walking home he saw Uncle Eddie working in his garden. Zeke yelled (from across the street); Zeke said: "Uncle Eddie, I just gave Bruiser his hat back. He was so happy; he's going to join the football team. I told him your story about the Caterpillar. I told him that he was in an 'ugly caterpillar' stage, but that he could become a beautiful butterfly. He said that I was the first person who was nice to him. I told him that he would be a great football player because he's so big & strong."

Eddie looked at Zeke then said: "That's wonderful news. You truly are a 'special and unique' child. I have another question for you." Zeke ran across the street to Eddie's house then said: "I hope that it's not another trick question or a question about caterpillar poop."

Eddie smiled (when Zeke said the phrase 'trick question or caterpillar poop), then Eddie said: "Zeke, is it better to live each day being afraid; or is it better to live each day of your life doing what you love?" Zeke looked at Eddie and said: "That's not a hard question. I think that I know the answer to that question. The answer is: 'You should always live each day doing what you love.' Why would you ask me that question?"

Eddie then said, "Many people live in fear. Many people are afraid to try and do what they love to do. Your brother Zack is a fearful person. Some people are afraid to get on airplanes. Some people want to be pilots, even though they might die in a plane crash. Some people are afraid of germs; and are reluctant to be around large groups of people.

During the 'CoronaVirus' Pandemic, the healthcare professionals told people to stay at least six feet away from each other and to avoid being in groups of ten or more people. This is very good advice during a 'contagious' virus outbreak; people were advised to increase their: 'social distance' --- keep at least 6 feet between each person. This is very good advice during a Virus outbreak, but many children today isolate themselves. Many children hide inside their homes and have very little social contact with other people. Many children today stare at their cell phones (most of the day) or they play games on their laptops. Children should be outdoors and enjoying Nature; like you and Billy."

Ralph Waldo Emerson said: "<u>It is not length of life, but depth of life</u>." Zeke looked at Eddie and said: "I don't know Mr. Emerson or what his saying means. Uncle Eddie, is Mr. Emerson a friend of yours? Does he live nearby? Is he a catalyst?"

Eddie smiled (as he thought about Zeke's questions), then said: "Mr. Emerson lived a long time ago, but was a wise man. I want to tell you a few stories that relate to his famous saying. I know that you will understand because you are a very good listener and very insightful.

My first story is about a dear friend of mine who died young. My friend was a teacher and a Nature lover; he especially loved birds. I think of him whenever song birds are in my yard. My friend used the outdoors as his classroom. He would often take his students to the nearby park to teach them about Nature and the 'diversity of life' that existed in the local park. My friend's name was Charlie.

Charlie's students learned to 'love Nature.' His students would work in groups while they were in the park woods. They would do Math activities, Social Studies activities, Science activities, Geography activities; they would also write poems, keep journals and identify plants & animals. He also taught them how to become 'good observers' --- they learned how to see - 'beauty in unusual places.'

Each group of students had an 'earth plot.' Their 'earth plot' was a small section of woods that contained a deciduous tree and a conifer tree. Each group would study and record how their 'earth plot' changed --- during the year.

The lower grade students couldn't wait to get to sixth grade and be in Mr. Charlie's class. Sixth grade in Charlie's town was every student's favorite year. All of the sixth graders loved walking to the park and doing their school work - in the outdoors.

Today, many of Charlie's former students are parents and some are grandparents, but they still go back into the park --- just to see their 'earth plots.' Many adults take their children and grandchildren into those park woods and say (to their little loved ones): 'This was my 'earth plot;' and these were my trees. I loved being in Mr. Charlie's class. Sixth grade was so much fun!'

But as I said, Charlie died young. Charlie used Nature to teach the academic skills that his students needed to learn. Charlie loved Nature but he also loved cigarettes. Charlie started smoking cigarettes when he was about fourteen. When he started smoking, grownups didn't know that cigarettes were a health hazard. Charlie got lung cancer and died a few weeks after learning he had cancer. He's been dead for almost 20 years but I still miss him. Every time that I see you and Billy playing catch, I think of Charlie. Charlie was a very good catcher and he almost made it to the Major Leagues. We were 'battery mates;' I was the pitcher and he was my catcher --- just like you and Billy are 'battery mates.' (i.e., pitcher & catcher). Little Zeke, don't ever start smoking cigarettes or vaping; vaping is even more dangerous. If you do, you will be killing yourself --- little by little."

Zeke looked at Eddie then said: "That's a sad story. I feel bad that you lost your good friend. I'm never going to smoke cigarettes or vape. Mr. Charlie must have been an Omega, since he loved Nature. I hope that I can have a Middle school teacher like Mr. Charlie, when I get to Middle School. Mr. Charlie must have been a 'catalyst' too."

Eddie looked at Zeke then said: "He was a 'positive catalyst.' He brightened the lives of all of his students and all of the adults who knew him. He was like you, Zeke, he could see beauty in tiny little places. But he was addicted to tobacco; he couldn't stop smoking cigarettes --- cigarettes took away my good friend.

Zeke, I'm telling you about Charlie because of the Emerson quotation that I told you ('It is not length of life, but depth of life'). As I told before, there are many mysteries in life. When my friend Charlie died, I was asked to speak at his funeral and I did. It was very difficult for me, but we were close friends. Shortly after Charlie died, I found an envelope in my mailbox. When I opened the envelope, I found a little Jingle shell. The Jingle seashell was glued to a piece of paper and on the paper was Emerson's saying: '<u>It is not length of life, but depth of life</u>.' I have no idea how that Jingle seashell got into my mailbox; it is still a mystery to me --- but I look at that Jingle shell and the saying everyday."

Zeke looked at Eddie then said: "I have a mystery to solve too. Mr. Hill has an 'egg-shaped' rock too. His rock is exactly like mine; it has the same lady's profile etched into it. Mr. Hill showed me a picture of the lady and told me her name. He told me that he and I are somehow connected. He told me that the lady (whose picture is in my rock) is named 'Bessie Hill.' He said that she died suddenly when she was young; she was only 37 when she died and that her two children became orphans. He hopes that I can solve the mystery of Bessie's sudden and suspicious death. He said that she was 'asphyxiated.' I told him that Nature will help me solve his mystery."

Eddie looked at me and said: "Wow! Asphyxiation! She was suffocated. That's horrible. That must have been horrible for her two children. Edna has a friend who is an expert at solving ancestry mysteries. Edna's friend's name is Norma. Norma has helped many people find out about their ancestors. Norma knows how to solve 'family ancestry mysteries.' I'm going to ask Norma to help you solve this mystery, but there is one more story that I wanted to tell you about.

This story is related to Emerson's quote, too. This story is about a little girl and her Middle School basketball coach. This little girl was a 'super athlete.' This little girl was the best athlete in the area, and she excelled in a lot of sports. The basketball coach is a friend of my nephew. The girl's name was Jo-Jo (that's not really her name), and the coach was called Mr. D.

This story could be titled: 'The Final Game.' Long ago, when the coach (Mr. D.) was approaching his final game, he told his players: 'Girls, as you know this is my last season of coaching. Girls, the team that we are going to play (tonight - in our final game) for the Championship has beaten us three (3) times this year. This is your last opportunity to beat this team. I'm sure that this team thinks that they will beat us (again) tonight, but I know that you have the ability to win. I'm also giving you 'a prize' that's never been given before. Then, the coach smiled and tugged on his beard. As an incentive, I told you that you could shave off my beard, if you win this Championship game. Then the girls held up their mothers' razors. The team of girls pointed their mothers' razors at the coach and smiled; then they said: 'Mr. D, you're going to lose your beard tonight.'

The coach had his beard for many years but was more than willing to sacrifice it. Then the coach said: 'Girls, you're going to win tonight if you play as a team and play defense - like I know that you can. Trust me, play hard and enjoy this moment! Then the coach gave another tug on his beard and smiled.'

The Championship game truly was an 'epic battle.' The other team was 'well coached,' disciplined and very physical. In the closing seconds of the game, Coach D's team was in the lead by two points. The opponent knew that they had to commit a foul (in order to stop the clock), so Jo-Jo was fouled. Before, shooting her 'foul shots,' Coach D said (to Jo-Jo): "Don't think. Just take a deep breath and shoot the ball --- don't think, just breathe then shoot!' Jo-Jo made those shots and the final buzzer went off. Coach D's team had done - what most believed couldn't be down. Now, they were ready for their prize.

As soon as the game ended, the players (from both teams) shook hands. The players (from the opposing team) were in tears. The boys' team was scheduled to play right after the girls' game, but the gym emptied.

As soon as the girls' game was over, all of the players and most of the fans left the gym. The players, and their coach (Mr. D) were in the Home Ec. classroom. Coach D. was sitting in a chair and the girls (fans and parents) were chanting: 'BYE! BYE! BEARD!' Then the fun (for the girls began). The girls took out shaving cream and lathered up the coach's beard. Then the girls (took turns); they shaved the coach's beard off. The coach's face had several 'nicks' & cuts, so the girls put bandaids on his cuts.

It was a night that will live on forever and was videotaped by many parents, but it was a 'bittersweet' night. Unbeknownst to the coach, this wasn't only his final game, it was Jo-Jo's final game. Jo-Jo never got to play basketball again; she had cancer and died of cancer. Jo-Jo never got to High School.

Zeke looked at Eddie then said: "Uncle Eddie, that's a very sad story. Why would you tell me such a sad story? I'm really confused." Eddie looked at Zeke and said, "Zeke, you are right. It is a very sad story. That coach will think of that little girl the rest of his life and I will think of my dear friend Charlie for the rest of my life. But the beauty of those two people, lives on in me and in coach D.   Charlie and Jo-Jo added beauty to the lives of others. Charlie's spirit lives on in me. I see him in the flowers, trees and in birds - especially when they sing.

Jo-Jo's & Charlie's lives were short (in length) but they had depth. Those two people were filled with joy and passion; they developed their 'innate gifts' and shared them with others. The life of Butterflies is very short, but they add beauty to everyone who gets to see them.   Giuseppe's first child died (from influenza) when he was only four (4) years old.

The length of a person's life is not important. What is important is: 'that we live each day - 'with depth!' Zeke, you do have 'depth' in your life: 1) you enjoy each day, 2) you are developing your talents, 3) you 'see' the beauty that is all around you, and 4) you share your 'joy-filled self' with everyone that you meet.

Some people are paralyzed by 'fear;' they might live a long life but they don't live, --- they exist. Your cranky neighbor is old but he isn't a happy person. He has a dog that's named 'Happy,' but he isn't happy. Zeke, never let 'fear' take away your joy; just keep being who you are.

Many people are afraid of the CoronaVirus. It is wise to take precautions to avoid or prevent becoming sick with the virus. But germs, and viruses CANNOT destroy the 'spirit or depth' of joy-filled people. The joy-filled people have learned (from Nature); they will adapt to any and all 'sudden life events.' The spirit of 'joy-filled' people continues on - in the lives of others (even after they die).

I think that 'fear' is the biggest 'killer' of life. Viruses cannot kill the 'human spirit' but fear can. Mr. Rogers has died but his spirit lives on. His special number: '143' lives in people like you. You demonstrated Mr. Roger's love of life when you gave Bruiser his hat back and befriended him. As Mr. Roger's said: 'Kindness is love --- in action.' Zeke, every day, I see Mr. Roger's spirit - living in you."

Zeke looked at Eddie then said: "Uncle Eddie, I like listening to your stories, but you talk like Mr. Hill. A lot of what you talk about is too difficult for me to understand ---

it's too deep (Ha! Ha!).   That's really sad about your friend Charlie, and Jo-Jo, and Giuseppe's son; but Billy just got home. I want to go exploring with Billy.

I won't be paralyzed by fear; my brother Zack is. He still thinks that there are monsters living under our beds and in our attic. I kinda like seeing my brother Zack being afraid, because he punches me a lot --- and it hurts! Thanks for talking to me! I really do like listening to your stories; you're a catalyst too. Bye Uncle Eddie!

****

22. The Final Analysis

The next day, when Zeke was walking over to Billy's house, he saw Uncle Eddie in front of his house. Eddie was talking to a man. Zeke yelled: "Hi Uncle Eddie!" Eddie responded, "Zeke, come here. I want you to meet my nephew."

Zeke ran across the street to Eddie's house and Eddie said, "Zeke, this is my nephew; his name is Butchie." Zeke looked at Butchie then said: "Hi Butchie. Uncle Eddie is very kind and he always gives me and Billy candy. He also has the greenest lawn in town." Butchie looked at Zeke then said, "Eddie does have the greenest lawn in town and he's my favorite uncle."

Zeke looked at Butchie then said: "Butchie is an unusual name. All of the people who have unusual names seem to be Omegans; are you an Omegan?" Butchie responded, "Butchie is my nickname, but I am an Omega. I love Nature and try to learn its secrets. I want to help make life on earth sustainable. Nature has all of the answers. My uncle Eddie taught me about the benefits of composting. I have a friend who grows vegetables in a greenhouse. My farmer friend grows Lettuce and he uses fish poop as fertilizer. He has fish in tanks and uses their waste water to water and fertilize his lettuce plants. When he puts clean water in his fish tanks he doesn't throw out the dirty waste water; he uses it to fertilize his lettuce plants. It truly is amazing. That kind of farming is called: "Aqua-ponics.""

Zeke looked at Butchie then said: "Wow! That is amazing! Billy and I got pooped on by caterpillars, when we were exploring in the woods. Caterpillar poop is disgusting. I like exploring and Nature leads me to its treasures."

Butchie looked at Zeke then said, "My uncle Eddie told me about some of your treasures. He sent me a picture of the Box turtle's shell and he sent me the phone that you found buried in a mud puddle. I came here today to tell Eddie that I got some answers about your treasures. Zeke, since you are here, I'll tell you what I found out. My professor friend said: 'that the barcode design on the turtle's shell is 'Mayan.' It is some kind of Mayan message. The professor is going to try and decipher it (figure out what it means). He knows that it's Mayan, but doesn't know what it means.

My computer friend decoded the binary numbers that were on the cellphone that you found. The encrypted message on your phone said: 'Bessie's sudden death was suspicious ...solve this mystery...it's in your DNA...you are connected to Bessie.' I have no idea who Bessie is." Zeke looked at Butchie then said: "Bessie is the lady whose picture is etched into my 'egg-shaped' rock. Let me show you my rock."

Zeke handed his 'egg-shaped' rock to Butchie, then heard a 'meowing' sound coming from Butchie's car. While Butchie was looking at Zeke's rock, Zeke saw a cat looking at him. The cat was inside of Butchie's car and looking at Zeke; it was meowing at Zeke. Then Zeke looked at Butchie and said: "Mr. Butchie, your cat is meowing at me. I can talk to animals. Animals understand what I'm saying when I talk to them. There's a special rabbit that lives in my yard and he smells like lavender. What is your cat's name?"

Butchie looked at Zeke, then said: "That's not my cat. I'm just watching my friend's cat this weekend. The cat's name is Chris. The cat showed up at my friend's house on Christmas Eve. The cat's back leg was mangled; it was injured. My friends (Art & Diane) took the cat to the Vet. The Vet had to amputate the cat's one leg.

Art and Diane adopted the cat and named it Chris, because he came to their house on Christmas Eve. Chris (the cat) is fine and functions well with 3 legs. It is amazing how animals can adapt. Art & Diane have two dogs (Millie & George). Millie and George don't like Chris (the cat). So Chris has his own pet door. Art made a pet door for Chris. Chris goes out the pet door in the morning and comes back inside at night. The pet door leads to the basement, so the dogs can't get to the cat. The dogs live upstairs (inside of the house) and the cat lives in the basement.

Art & Diane are animal lovers. They have several horses and they rescue dogs. They are: 'dog & cat transport volunteers.' When cats or dogs are rescued and need to be given rides to their new adoption site, Art & Diane drive them to the next animal shelter; sometimes they foster dogs too (care for dogs for a few weeks; until the shelter finds a new owner)."

Zeke looked at Butchie then said: "Art and Diane must be nice people. They must be Omegans too, if they like animals. Mr. Butchie, I want to give you my newest treasure. I want to give you my fossil rock. Mr. Henry found treasures when he was digging a grave and one of the treasures is a rock with a fossil in it. I think it may be a Dinosaur fossil. Maybe your professor friend can find out if it's a Dinosaur and what kind of Dinosaur fossil it is. I'm going to run home and get my fossil rock."

Butchie looked at Zeke and said, "Zeke, I have to take my friend to the airport. My friend is a Marine Biologist and is going on a research expedition. He wants to help the ocean ecosystem and save the Coral Reefs. The Coral reefs are disappearing because the oceans are becoming more acidic. The oceans are absorbing Carbon Dioxide and creating carbonic acid. The Carbonic acid is also hurting Oysters. The acid is preventing the baby Oysters from making their shells. The baby Oysters can't survive without a shell. My friend is an expert on pearls and Oysters. He told me that he was a supervisor in a Pearl factory. After I pick up my friend, I'll stop back; Eddie's house is on the way to the airport. You can give me your fossil rock when I get back."

When Butchie drove away, Zeke went home and got his fossil rock. Zeke walked back to Eddie's house; he was hoping that Butchie would come soon. While Zeke was waiting for Butchie he asked Eddie about acid destroying the Coral Reefs. Eddie looked at Zeke and said, "Zeke, there are acids and bases. Sour things, like lemons, have acid in them. Carbon is the big problem for Coral and many animals. If we can lessen the amount of Carbon that's in the air, we can save the Coral Reefs and many other animals." Zeke looked at Eddie then said: "I want to help the Coral Reefs; what can I do?"

Eddie looked at Zeke and held up an acorn. Then Eddie said, "This little acorn holds the answer. The Earth's climate is warming. The more Carbon Dioxide that's in the air the warmer the Earth will get. The oceans are absorbing that carbon dioxide and it is affecting Coral, Oysters and many other animals in the ocean. We need to keep the Carbon Dioxide out of the ocean; we need to lock up the Carbon Dioxide."

Zeke responded, "Uncle Eddie, how can you lock up Carbon Dioxide? Can you see it? Can you capture it and lock it up?" Eddie responded, "No, you can't see it. When people exhale (breathe out), Carbon Dioxide goes into the air. The green plants need Carbon Dioxide; plants use it to make sugar. So if you plant trees, they will take the Carbon Dioxide out of the air and 'lock it up;' the Carbon will be stored in the wood of trees. The little acorn will grow into a giant Oak tree. The giant Oak trees can keep the Carbon 'locked up' for hundreds of years. If everybody would bury acorns like a squirrel does, we will have millions of Oak trees. When I die, I don't want a Memorial Bench; I want my loved ones to bury acorns in sunny fields or in a sunny place in their yard."

Zeke looked at Eddie and said: "Uncle Eddie, I don't want you to die. But I can and will start to bury acorns. I want to help save the Coral Reefs." Then Zeke heard meowing. Zeke looked and saw Butchie. Butchie was holding Chris (the 3 legged cat). Zeke said to Butchie, "Can Chris walk with 3 legs?" Butchie looked at Zeke then said, "Sure he can; watch!" Butchie put Chris down on the ground and Chris started meowing. Zeke meowed back at Chris, and Chris ran up to Zeke and hopped onto Zeke's lap. Zeke then said to Butchie: "That's amazing! Chris can run and jump and he only has 3 legs."

Butchie then said, "Plants and animals know how 'adapt.' Zeke, my friend has a gift for you. My friend goes by the name of 'J.' My friend has heard about this little boy named Zeke and his 'unique' connection to Nature." I'm taking 'J' to the airport, but he wanted to give you this box. He wouldn't tell me what's in it. He said that you would know and understand --- when you look inside the box."

Then 'J.' got out of Butchie's car and walked up to Zeke and said: "Hi Little Zeke, you will know how to open this box. You will see me again, one day. Continue to explore and 'see' all of Nature's beauty. Let Nature 'teach' you so that you can teach others how to 'live and how to treat Nature.' Nature needs your help." Then 'J.' handed Zeke a beautiful 'wooden treasure box.' Then 'J' touched Zeke on the arm and walked away. Before driving off, 'J' said: "Just continue being your 'natural self.' All people should be like you." Then Butchie and 'J' drove away.

Eddie looked at the wooden box that Zeke was holding and said, "Wow! That is a beautiful treasure box. How are you going to open it; it's locked!" Zeke looked at Eddie then said: "The lock has an Omega symbol next to it. I have a 'special' Omega skeleton key. I know that my key will open this box."

Zeke took out his skeleton key and placed it into the lock hole. Zeke's key fit perfectly. Zeke turned his key and the box opened. On the inside top cover was the following engraving: 'A teacher affects eternity; he can never tell where his influence stops.' - Henry Adams

Then Zeke saw a velvet 'cinch pouch.' The pouch had the initials 'J.E.D.' monogrammed on it. Zeke opened the velvet pouch and found several hand-written notes and he also found a smaller pouch. When Zeke opened the smaller pouch he found 7 pearls and a note that said: 'Little Zeke, you will know who to give these pearls to.' As soon as Zeke picked up the pearls he could feel his hands getting 'warm & tingly.' Inside the small pouch was also an acorn and a Jingle shell. The Jingle seashell was glued onto a piece of 'parchment paper' and it had the following quote: 'It is not length of life, but depth of life. - Ralph Waldo Emerson

Zeke turned and looked at Eddie then said: "Uncle Eddie, these are healing pearls. I have to give these to Mr. Ben. Mr. Ben makes healing necklaces for children who are sick." Zeke then handed the pearls to Eddie and said: "Uncle Eddie, tell me what you feel when you hold these pearls." Eddie held the pearls in his hand and said, "Zeke, these pearls are beautiful and they make my hand feel 'warm & tingly."

Zeke just smiled, then Zeke took out the other notes that were in the treasure box. One note said: 'Let Nature teach you; it has all of the answers. Then you can teach others how to live. Remember, 'Example is the best teacher.' You are a 'Great Example' --- of Mr. Roger's special #143. Zeke, you are an example of 'love;' your acts of kindness are - 'love in action.' KINDNESS is 'LOVE --- in action!

As Zeke continued to study his treasure box he noticed some other engravings. Engraved into the wood were: Ps 118:24 and 1C 13:4-7 and 1C 13:13

Zeke knew that those engravings were coded messages, but he was clueless; he had no idea what they could mean. But Zeke also believed that Nature would lead him to the answers.

Before reading the next hand-written note, Zeke decided to read the framed letter. There was a beautiful letter that was inside of a glass frame. The typed letter was titled: <u>The Final Analysis</u> and it said:

"<u>The Final Analysis</u>"
People are often unreasonable, illogical and self-centered,
Forgive them anyway.
If you are kind, people may accuse you of selfish ulterior motives;
Be kind anyway.
If you are successful, you will win some false friends and some enemies,
Succeed anyway.
If you are honest and frank, people will cheat you;
Be honest and frank anyway.
What you spend years building, someone may destroy overnight;
Build anyway.
If you find serenity and happiness, they may be jealous;
Be happy anyway.
The good that you do today, people will often forget tomorrow;
Do good anyway.
Give the world the best that you have and it may not be enough;
Give the world the world the best you've got anyway.
You see, in the <u>final analysis</u>, it is all between you and God.
<u>It was never between you and them anyway</u>.

-   Mother Teresa of Calcutta   -

After reading that framed letter, Zeke looked at Eddie and said: "Uncle Eddie, do you understand what that letter means? And do you know who Mother Teresa is? Is she Teresa's mother? Is she one of Butchie's friends?

Eddie looked at Zeke and said, "Mother Teresa was a religious Nun. She devoted her life to taking care of the poorest of poor people. She was a very special lady, but is no longer alive. Her kindness still lives on --- in people like you."

Then Zeke looked at another hand-written note (in the treasure box). This note started with Emerson's quotation: "Adopt the pace of Nature, her secret is patience." Then it said: 'Your brother Zack has very little patience - Zeke, you have a lot of patience. The Earth has been revolving around the Sun for billions of years; the seasons come and go. Nature continues to adapt and change. Humans and Human Empires have tried to control Nature --- they have failed. Nature will never be controlled. Nature will adjust & adapt to everything that humans do.

Omegans (Nature lovers) and 'kind & caring' humans will help make the 'Living Earth' sustainable. Nature will NEVER be controlled --- Omegans know this!

After reading this note, Zeke folded it up. When Zeke began to fold the note, he noticed tiny printing on the back of the note. Zeke decided to look at the 'tiny printing' through his green sea glass (his sea glass magnified things). When Zeke looked through his seaglass he could read the note. The note said: 'I am not a religious person because of what happened to me when I was little; but a religious Nun gave me the framed note. Even though I'm not religious, I believe this letter and I wanted you to have a copy --- because you will understand it and live by what it says. The nun who gave me the framed letter said her name was Sister Joy. She said that her name ('Joy,' which is the religious name that she chose), is an acronym. Zeke, the name that I'm writing at the end of this note is an acronym too.

'In conclusion, Zeke --- 'joy-filled' life is very simple; just be 'yourself.' Zeke, you are able to see beauty in tiny little things. Nature will continue to display her beauty to you (and all). Keep exploring and creating 'joy-filled memories' with your friends. And keep aiding Nature and those in need --- it is in your Nature. Show all that you meet how to treat Nature and each other; you are able to make others feel --- 'more beautiful inside.' Again, just be your 'natural self/'

Sincerely,
JABU

Zeke looked at Eddie then said: "Uncle Eddie, what is an 'acro-name?' Eddie looked at Zeke and said, "I think, you mean the word acronym. An acronym is a word where each letter in the word means something. The word Scuba is an acronym; it means: 'Self contained underwater breathing apparatus.' Zeke, Butch's professor friend gave you a lot of stuff to look at & think about. For some reason, I think that he knows you. Something is telling me that he knows you; especially when I read what he wrote in those notes."

Zeke looked at Eddie then said: "Mr J. sure did give me a lot of nice things. This treasure box is beautiful. I'm going to keep all of my treasures in this beautiful box. I can lock it too, because I have a special Omega Skeleton key." Eddie looked at Zeke and said, "I can't believe that you had a key to open that box. I wonder how Mr. J. would know that you had that key."

Zeke looked at Eddie then said: "Uncle Eddie, that's a good point; how would Mr. J. know that I had the key to open his treasure box? I'm going to go home and think about all the stuff that's in this treasure box. Bye Uncle Eddie! Your nephew Butchie is really nice; he's a lot like you."

When Zeke got home, he took his new treasure box up to his bedroom. Then Zeke took out his other notes; he was going to put his first notes (Mr. Hill's note and the note from 'the thing') into his new treasure box.

When Zeke looked at 'the thing's' note and Mr. J's note, he noticed that the handwriting was the same. Then Zeke began to read the note from 'the thing,' the thing's note said: "LIttle boy, I'm OK. I was the boy who disappeared on the beach long ago. Nature knew that I needed help. Nature rescued me. As a child, I was abused. Then Nature rescued me...One day I will leave this safe place....You will meet me one day, and you will know that it is me. You will know that it is me - when I touch your arm." This last sentence made Zeke have a 'flashback.'

Suddenly, Zeke realized that Mr. J. was 'the thing.' Zeke knew that Mr.J. was the thing because of: how it felt when Mr. J. touched his arm - before he left for the airport. Uncle Eddie's nephew (Butchie) told Zeke that Mr. J. was going on a Science Expedition. Mr. J. would be away for two (2) years. He would be trying to save the Coral Reefs. Zeke knew that two years is a long time --- especially to little boys.

Zeke knew that tonight he would be dreaming about two acro-names (acronyms); he would be trying to determine what 'JOY" and 'JABU' could mean. It didn't take long for Zeke to fall asleep tonight. Zeke was asleep & dreaming within one minute. But before falling asleep he heard the same night time noise. Zeke heard screaming from downstairs. A loud noise (from downstairs) was saying: "Zeke! Zeke! Did the monsters get you? Answer me!" Yep, Zeke's older (but scaredy cat) brother Zack was yelling to Zeke, but Zeke was already asleep and dreaming.

The life of Little boys - who are explorers --- is a: 'WONDERFUL LIFE!'

****

Postscript

In this volume, you learned more about the 'life journey' of two little brothers. Those two brothers were only one year apart (in age), but were very different. One brother (Zack) was often in trouble, or doing something mischievous. The younger brother (Zeke) was quiet, and shy. Zeke also had a 'unique' connection to Nature.

Like all children, Zeke loved to explore. But unlike most children, Zeke could: 'see' - 'beauty' --- in tiny little things. Zeke was able to 'see' --- 'goodness' and was blessed with a: 'forgiving heart' --- Zeke forgave and aided: 'Bullies.' Zeke was also able to 'communicate' with animals.

We (all) are on a 'life journey.' We (all) are stuck on Planet Earth and are zooming through space while orbiting our ruler --- 'The Sun.' As we journey through life we should scatter: 'love and kindness.' As R. L. Stevenson said: "Don't judge each day by what you reap, but by what you sow. " To that I would add: "Daily, sow: 'love & kindness.'

Everyone should try to be like Mr. Henry. Every neighborhood needs a Mr. Henry. And as James Barrie said: "Those who bring sunshine into the lives of others cannot keep it from themselves." <u>Kindness truly is a bridge between all people</u>.

It is the writer's hope that you (the reader) will let Nature 'teach you' (show you) how to live. Nature has the answer to every human dilemma (or situation). Nature does not waste energy. Nature just does what is needed and it does it effortlessly. As Emerson said: "Adopt the pace of Nature, her secret is patience."

The writer hopes that you (the reader) will try to make life on Earth sustainable. Earth Day is Celebrated on April 22nd. Everyday should be Earth Day! Everyday, we should do what we can to improve the 'quality of life' for the Earth's ecosystems and for our neighbors. Please, remember and live by the Indian Proverb: "We do not inherit the land from our ancestors, we borrow it from our children."

Please <u>Volunteer</u>! Everyone can add: 'Sunshine' - to their neighborhood. If you volunteer your time (to things that you care about), you will be 'brightening & enriching' people's lives; you also will feel --- 'more beautiful inside.'

Take time to enjoy Nature and take time to create joy-filled memories with your loved ones. Let Nature show you how to become --- 'more beautiful inside!' And as you live each day, remember my motto: "<u>Laugh, Smile and Be Kind.</u>"

Sincerely,
John Ezekial DeAngelis

(long, long ago --- Little Zeke)